# The Stories of Sister Sarah

*The Unholy Trinity – Volume 1*

David Clark

# The Stories of Sister Sarah

*Ghost Island*

David Clark

# 1

"First, I want to thank you for agreeing to meet with us."

The old woman sat upright in a simple wooden chair with a pleasant look on her face. A man, only a few years younger than her, sat off to her left. He was apprehensive and sat on the edge of his chair as if he were ready to pounce on some great evil at any moment. Looking at the tone of his senior-citizen body, it was obvious he could still do that if needed. He had every appearance of someone who knew a life of manual labor. Maybe a craftsman or a farmer. On either side of the woman's chair, two nuns knelt and prayed silently.

"Oh, not at all. I am more than happy to talk about my life. You will have to excuse my brother, he is a bit protective of me."

"Well, I hope to put him at ease. We are here with all due respect, and hope to conduct this interview as such. Your Mother Superior gave us an hour, shall we begin?"

The young man who had been speaking leaned forward just a bit further and placed a microphone on the floor in front of the elder nun. His black-rimmed glasses almost slipped off his nose when he bent over, prompting a quick push back into place with his forefinger. The hand continued to brush a mop of straggly-length dark hair out of his face.

"Any background?", he asked the blonde twenty-something to his side. The man gave him a thumbs up.

"First, can you introduce yourself and tell us who you are?"

"Sure, I am Sarah Meyer. Daughter of Edward Meyer."

"And, you are a nun here at San Francesco?"

"In a way of speaking. They take care of us, and I follow their beliefs and life. I must admit, I found the life very pleasing and finally took the oath when I was thirty-three."

"And how old are you? If you don't mind me asking?"

There was a great pause between the six people in the room, only the two nuns continued. Their prayers nothing more than a whisper.

"Not at all, I am 85 years old, and IT is 3184 years old."

One of the two nuns gasped out loud and paused her prayer for only the briefest of moments. Sarah looked in her direction and said with a calm voice,

"Please don't stop child. I don't want it to make a mess of these nice men. I have a story to tell."

There were two audible gulps in the room, and Jacob leaned forward further in his chair. Sarah extended her hand out toward her brother and placed it on his knee. She smiled rather mischievously. Not like someone who was evil, but more like someone who was having a little fun. Which was the case. At this moment, she felt in complete control of herself. The two younger nuns, both relatively new when compared to her length of stay, were doing a fine job of keeping Abaddon hidden, as did all the sisters that had served at Sarah's side. There were only brief moments where she lost control. All brought back under control without any world-ending catastrophes. A welcome improvement over the first time he took control of Sarah.

"You gentlemen can relax. We are perfectly fine at this moment, but let's not waste time."

"Yes ma'am. We don't want to cover what happened before you arrived here. We have already spoken to your brother about that, and that has been well documented many times over once the story came out."

Sarah chuckled, almost a grandmotherly laugh as if a grandchild amused her, but it came across as disturbing and, once again, set the tense room on edge. "Oh, I am sorry," she apologized. "I don't know why, can't really explain it, but thinking about how our secret was let out still amuses me. Maybe it was how hard everyone worked to keep it a secret, but in the end the Vatican published a book on us all. No investigative exposé or anything, just a book all on our own."

"Yes," he stumbled. "It is a wonderful book. I have read it many times. The section on you and your family is fascinating."

"I have read it too. They missed quite a bit, but that is expected. Please continue."

"What we are most interested in are the stories once you arrived here. The, I guess, cases you helped Father Lucian and the other keepers with through the years, using.. ITs power."

"I imagined that was what you would want to hear. I helped him with a great many, up until his passing, and then Father Domingo took his place and we continued our work. Is there a particular one you want to hear about first?"

He consulted his notebook, flipping through several pages of scribbled items. Sarah thought, *how old school of him, he still writes notes.* Most of those that have come and talked to her walked in with a digital notebook or robotic camera. Not these two. The main interviewer, a man in his mid-thirties she would guess, in a brown sweater almost has that documentary film student look, with his pad full of notes. She bet, and before she finished the thought, her eyes found the pencil stuck behind his ear. During the vetting process, something Jacob always did, he verified these two were not just students, or anyone that might be there to exploit her. They were professionals, two of the best. Ralph Fredricks, and two-time Golden Globe winner, and his cameraman Kenneth Lloyd. Sarah hadn't had a chance to watch any of the films they produced, but she trusted her brother. She was aware of the sheer number that he had turned down since the book came out fifteen years ago.

The book, something no one warned anyone about, was aimed at trying to return the world's faith in the spiritual. Pope Mark, a priest from Columbia, said he felt like he was watching the world walk away from God and toward the digital spark of technology, forgetting who they really were and where they came from. It was a theme in every sermon he gave. It was also dead center of his policies and directions from the Papal office. A media campaign, unlike any the church had undertaken, began to show the world the spiritual side they had forgotten. Movies and shows about religious sites and figures. The reception was lukewarm. His critics within the church said the stories were old and worn. Everyone knew the figures. Everyone knew the sites. None of them had any appeal.

Then, through several edicts and Papal papers, he began to acknowledge the church's belief in the paranormal, and the truth about its support in the practice of exorcisms. Both were expected to make a splash, but they didn't do much more than create a ripple. Popular culture movies and themes had desensitized the entire world to those topics. In what some called an act of desperation, he outed the Sites, the Keepers, and all their stories. To Sarah's horror, there was no warning when it was released. Mother Francine woke her early one morning and told her as soon as she had heard herself. That was the first. She lived in fear for a while, and stayed secluded in her room. Not even taking the walks out among the trees in the courtyards to listen to the birds, an activity she had grown very fond of through the years. Sarah knew some details of her story were not as glorious as others, and might even make her the target for both those wanting to grab a piece of story, and those that would fear her and want to protect the world from her, but no one came. No one inquired. The public dismissed the stories as works of fiction. Then little by little, a few interviews with keepers here and a documentary there, credibility grew. That created a ground swell which turned into a tidal wave of requests. All of which the Abbey diverted to Jacob, who eagerly volunteered so they wouldn't be bothered. It was a burden he explained he needed to do after all they had done for his sister.

"Sister, how about the first time?" Ralph asked, after closing his notebook.

"How did I know you would ask about Poveglia?"

"It is called the most haunted place in the world, and it was your first time," he responded.

"Well, then. Let's get to it."

# 2

Six months had passed since Sarah first joined the sisters at San Francesco. So far, they had kept everything under control, and she was adjusting to life at the Abbey. It was quiet, pleasant, and most importantly, secluded. With spring setting in, she took full advantage of the wooded courtyard in the back to enjoy the sun and the songbirds that made their homes in the trees. She enjoyed the walks, and had grown used to her escorts who were never far behind.

The days were routine, which was fine with her. There was a calm and peaceful feel to them. Each morning, prayer, breakfast, more prayer, and a morning session with Mother Demiana. Those sessions covered how she was feeling, the ever-present being that was in there with her, and some were just chats. Prior to visiting the Vatican for her training, Sarah had never seen or spoken to an honest-to-goodness nun. Every opinion she had was based on television or movies. The ones she met there were rather reserved, and fit those opinions. The ones she now called family were rather normal. They were devout and dedicated, there was no doubt in that, but they were personable. Mother Demiana was not the strict Mother Superior you saw in movies. She was caring and nurturing to her sisters and the surrounding community, which they were all openly involved with. Well, all except Sarah.

The sisters spent the afternoons out among the community, delivering prayers to the sick, teaching, and just being part of a community. Sarah's charitable contribution was limited to putting together care packages, preparing meals for the hungry, and helping to organize classes for the local children. All of which she could do from inside the confines of the Abbey. This was at Sarah and Mother Demiana's request. Sarah was still leery about being out around people with what all had happened. Inside, she didn't think she would ever be able to just go out in the town like the others. Mother Demiana was cautious, but believed, with time, she would join the others.

It was during one of those afternoons while she was helping to bake loaves of bread in the kitchen when Sister Claudia told her she had a visitor. Something that was common for the first few months as Jacob took every opportunity he could to come see her, but he had left for home three months ago. So this was curious. She followed her through the corridor to the front to see who that might be. Her escort followed just feet behind her, the prayer never stopped. Sarah wondered if her father had come again to see her, something he had done once already, which was truly wonderful. Seeing him brought great joy to her heart. Being a keeper, he was also a little of a celebrity among the other sisters, which Sarah enjoyed. If it was him, this would be a surprise. She had just spoken to him the night before, and he had said nothing about being in Italy.

She heard Mother Demiana's voice coming down the hall. It carried a tone of worry, which transferred into Sarah. Was this bad news? Had something happened to her father or Jacob? When she rounded the corner and saw who was standing there, it added to it. Father Lucian hadn't visited since he escorted her here. This wasn't good.

"Sarah," he said as he embraced her. "It is good to see you again."

"What's wrong?"

"My dear, why would anything be wrong?" he asked.

"I heard Mother Demiana. She sounded worried," replied Sarah. She looked and gave a respectful nod to the Mother.

"It's only a disagreement. Shall we take a walk?"

Sarah looked at the Mother for approval, which she gave with a simple nod and smile, and then left her in the company of Father Lucian, who motioned for her to lead the way. If they were to take a walk, the halls are too narrow. The courtyard was nothing more than a place to sit. To Sarah, there was only one choice, and she led him out to the surrounding woods, a favorite of hers.

When they emerged out the back rod-iron gate, he moved up beside her. Together they stepped into what Sarah had called Eden. In the spring and summer, it was just cool enough to enjoy outside, no matter the time of day. During the fall and winter, the olive trees kept their leaves, and the sun provided just enough warmth to fight away any chill. The evergreen state and regulated temperature made it a haven for birds all year round, which filled the air with a symphony of nature. It was a place where Sarah enjoyed pleasant strolls, or even a moment to sit and read in the peaceful surroundings.

Today, it was just like the other days. Warm, but not too warm. Cool, but not too cool. Nature's orchestra rode the wind along with the sweet fragrance of the olive groves. As many times as she stepped into this world, it always felt as special as the first time. The awe of it seemed to overwhelm Father Lucian as well. He looked around for several minutes and finally spoke once they were deep in the trees.

"Sarah, how are you, child?"

"I am good, Father. I am adjusting. How have you been?"

"Fine, just fine. Things have been a bit quieter lately. I am not complaining, mind you. It is all part of the ebb and flow of the universe. Peace and conflict. As always, conflict will return soon enough."

"Have you talked to my father and Jacob recently?"

"I have a couple of times," he told her. "Jacob was a quick study, and is now working with his father. He is always interested in my evaluation of his decisions though. He needs to trust his own judgement more. Maybe that is something you can mention to him the next time you talk to him."

"I will," she said. Hearing of his requests for feedback didn't surprise her. Everything he did for the last several years, from sports to school, had been followed with some form of evaluation, some form of debriefing with a coach or his father. Sarah thought about her own time after returning from her training, and didn't remember ever reaching out to Father Lucian, her own father, or even Father Murray. Why was that? She didn't know for sure, but hazarding her own guess, it had something to do with the creature inside her. Maybe IT was providing the encouragement and confirmation. "I speak to them often. I guess he looks at you like he does his baseball coach, or did."

"Ah, yes, baseball. I was as surprised as I imagine you were, when he gave all that up to reopen the family farm."

"Surprise is not a strong enough word, Father. In the world over there, farming is not really considered an exciting or cool profession. So hearing a teenager say he wants to be a farmer is a little, well, shocking, but I will say this. Jacob has always been deliberate with everything he has done. I am sure he has thought this out," Sarah paused and swallowed hard before asking a question that had been on her mind for months. When she asked her father, he changed the subject. She hoped Father Lucian would be truthful with her. "How are things there? Any more problems?"

"All is quiet. Just the occasional spirit that has always passed through there. Nothing your father and brother can't handle. I know why you ask, and Sarah, you need to clear your mind. You are not responsible for what happened. You need to rid yourself of that burden you feel."

"I know, Father. I just don't know how." This was a frequent topic between Mother Demiana and Sarah. Advice ranged from repenting and praying, to working with the community, something Sarah didn't feel comfortable with yet. Sarah had tried all the praying and inspirational readings she could find, something she still spent an hour or more on each day. Some gave her perspective. Told her of historical figures that paid a harsh price. Others were just stories that all seemed to focus on the same topic. 'God gives us the burden we are able to bear'. Maybe that was the simple truth in all this for Sarah. Something inside her had the strength to bear this burden, this weight. If that was the case, she knew she would have to just accept it, but she couldn't help but to think there was something more to it.

"I might be able to help with that. Remember what I asked you after I told you about how life would have to be now?"

"You mean about helping you?", asked Sarah. A quizzical smile spread across her face.

"Yes, that is what me and the Mother were talking about when you walked up. I have a place I want to take you and get your input on, but she thinks it is too soon."

Too soon, was what Sarah thought too. She still hadn't ventured down the winding path that led up to the Abbey from the town. The walls of this place provided a comfort that if something happened, they could handle it. The thought of going anywhere else was frightening.

"So, Sarah, what do you think? Would you like to come with me? It is just for a few days and it isn't too far away either."

"Father," she started, trying to sound strong and confident. "I appreciate the offer. I am just not sure this is the best time... the best time for me that is. I don't feel ready."

He moaned an inquisitive sound. "Mother tells me you haven't had any issues or relapses since you arrived. That is true, isn't it?"

"It is. I just don't want to press my luck. This place has really helped me there."

Father Lucian stopped in a particularly beautiful clearing in the trees. Splashes of sunshine rained through the foliage creating rays of brilliance. "God is the ultimate painter, isn't he Sarah?"

She had to agree, it was one of the most amazing sights she had ever seen. Even the particles of dust that danced in the wind looked brilliant as they glinted in the sunbeams.

Father Lucian walked to the center of the clearing and turned back to Sarah. "You haven't had any issues since you arrived here because of your faith and the faith of the sisters that have been protecting you. They will always be a fixture in your life, from now until your last days in this realm. After that, our Father will take care of you. You are one of his very special children, and Sarah, it is time you start on your true path. Trust me on this. We will take two of the sisters with us and will only be a few hours away. If anything at all happens, them and I can help put things right, and we will rush you back here, but that won't be necessary. Will you go?"

Feeling he wouldn't take no for an answer, she could only answer a very reluctant, "Sure."

# 3

Sarah's sleep was restless that night. Several dreams shook her awake, which wasn't uncommon. Images of the past usually invaded her mind when her conscious gave way to the world of the subconscious. That was why Mother Demiana arranged for three sisters to sit in Sarah's chambers while she slept. Those images were a little more active on this particular night. They came more frequently than most. Her cries-out occurred more often as well. Each time she woke, the praying continued, and she went back to sleep, comforted that they were watching over her. Even with their presence, she dreaded the nights. The fear Abaddon would strike while she wasn't aware of him enough to stop him always sat there. It was one reason she believed the images came so frequently while she slept. It was either IT, taking advantage of her state, or her worry.

The dawn brought the end of the concern. Well, maybe not completely, but it pushed it to the back of her mind while she was in control. This morning was different, a little of that concern hung around the knock on her chamber door. Outside, Mother Demiana and two sisters waited for her. Sarah took the last bite of her breakfast and then exited out the door, leaving her three night time protectors behind as two others took up the task.

"Morning, Mother," Sarah said.

"Morning, Sarah," she replied with a quick embrace. This is one of the few differences in the relationship between her and Sarah and her and the other sisters. Sarah always felt she was more motherly, or grandmotherly, toward her. She had seen the mother superior in her come out a few times when questions of faith came up. Something Sarah still found necessary to question to further her understanding. Each time, Mother Demiana responded with quick, but firm, affirmation and direction. "Well, let's not keep him waiting."

The four walked out the front gate and down the winding path. This was only Sarah's second time on this path. This time one black SUV, not two, waited for them at the bottom of the path. Father Lucian stood outside the passenger door.

Her two escorts loaded into the back. Before Sarah joined them, she asked, "Where are we going?"

Father Lucian's answer was just a single word, "Venice."

Being out and driving through the Italian countryside was nice and, in a way, renewed Sarah. It showed her there was a big world out there, beyond the walls of the Abbey. The world still stood, and the sun still shined on everyone else as they went about their business. Speeding through the small villages, she saw families out for a walk, people carrying bags of produce, bought at the local market, and others enjoying a mid-morning breakfast at an outdoor café. All smiling. All talking, with some laughing. Sarah tried to remember the last time she'd laughed with her family. Obviously it had been a while, but then she remembered. She had laughed with Mother Demiana. Oh, and Sister Julia, who, if there was a clown of the Abbey, looked for any moment for some humorous levity, it was her. They were her family now.

Over the next hour, clouds rolled in, allowing only a spot or two of sunlight every once in a while. Occasionally a light mist filled the air, but people were still out going about their business. They just moved in a hurry to get inside while using a hand or jacket to shield themselves from the rain. It continued that way into Venice, which Sarah first spotted from afar, and watched as the city grew in the front windscreen.

They drove across the long bridge to the main part of the city and, much to her disappointment, stayed to the south side of it, which had a more industrial feel to it, as this was where the main port for the area was located. To her left, she still saw signature stone buildings with red-tiled roofs. To her right, nothing but train tracks and large ships. Ahead of them, the open blue green water of the Venetian Lagoon. Their SUV pulled to a stop at the end of the road.

Father Lucian was the first to get out. Then he opened the back door for Sarah and her escorts. It wasn't raining at that moment, but the puddles on the ground gave every sign it had recently. He led them to the edge of the concrete wharf where a single rail sat up above the edge. He stepped over the edge and then down a few feet. Sarah approached and looked over the edge cautiously. Still not sure where they were going, and not seeing where he stepped, Sarah was left to wonder if he could walk on water. To her relief, a single set of metal stairs waited for them just beyond the edge. They led down to a floating dock with a small aluminum-bottomed boat moored to it. The boat bobbed up and down next to the dock in the rough surf, occasionally smacking it with a bang. Father Lucian stepped over into the boat and looked back at Sarah, who still hadn't taken her first step over the edge and onto the stairs. The rust spots she saw on the grated surfaces concerned her. On faith, she took the step with her right hand firmly on the rail to steady herself. It was a good thing too. The stairs moved up and down as the floating dock below it moved. That made her knees weak and wobbly, and she hoped stepping back on the firm dock would settle her down a little, but it was worse. There was no handrail to steady herself with each bob and drop of the dock.

With hands outstretched to either side, like someone walking a thin balance beam, Sarah walked down the ten-foot-wide dock to the boat and accepted the hands of both the captain and Father Lucian. Then stepped up and over the side of the boat. The other two sisters followed, neither as tentative as Sarah.

"So, where are we going?", Sarah asked. She scanned the horizon through the clouds and the fog and saw nothing out there.

"A small island, Poveglia, in the lagoon."

At that moment, both of the sisters seated next to Sarah paused ever so subtly. Their eyes trained on Father Lucian, who, with his hand urged both to calm down.

"Father, what is this place?", Sarah asked. "What aren't you telling me? The sisters seemed frightened by that name."

"Sarah, its nothing to worry about. It's not much more than an old ghost story that most in Italy know."

Sarah knew of the dedication of these sisters. She also knew about the strength of their faith. Why did that name startle them so much? "Father, what is this place?", she asked again.

The last line that moored the boat in place was cast off, and they pulled away from the dock and smoothly headed out into the fog. The boat rolled with the chop. Sarah noticed the captain steered with one hand on the wheel and the other on the throttle, adjusting it a little up and down with the conditions. Something she appreciated. Her father and Lewis Tillingsly once took her and Jacob out fishing in the James River. Lewis was at the helm and ran the boat at two speeds, coasting and full out. It was a tooth clattering ride against the chop at full throttle, and her and Jacob had to hold on for dear life. They were tossed up and then slammed back into their seat each time the bottom of the boat crashed into the crest of a wave. She imagined it would be much the same if the captain increased speed much more than it already was.

"Think about it as the Italian version of the Legend of Sleepy Hollow," continued Father Lucian.

"So the stories are all made up?", asked Sarah.

"Okay, that might not have been the best example. It really is nothing to worry about. The stories, like many things in life, are worse than the truth."

"Then let's hear some stories. It seems we have the time."

"Raccontale del campanile," said the captain, a rather young man that Sarah would guess was only a few years older than herself. He was tall and thin, with dark hair that hung in his face. Despite his young age, she could tell he had spent most of his life on or around the water. His legs worked as shock absorbers to the rocking motion. They were in constant motion to stabilize him, while the upper part of his torso never moved.

One of the many things Sarah had spent some time studying on upon her arrival was improving both her Latin and Italian. Neither were conversational, at least not yet. She had hopes that her Italian would get there soon, which meant she knew most of the words, just didn't always put them together in the correct way to form a sentence that wouldn't make the person listening look at her oddly. She recognized each of those words. A quick glance at her escorts told her they did as well. "What about the bell tower?" she asked. Just as two islands came into view, but the captain made no attempt to steer toward either.

"No. I want your honest readings and impression of this place, so I am not telling you anything. You just need to trust me."

They continued on for another fifteen minutes, and with nothing in sight, the tone of the engine slowed. Sarah peered through the fog that had become denser, and then it appeared. First an island covered in trees, then a second with a dock extending out into the lagoon. The second one had buildings on it, and towering high above the structures was a tall stone bell tower.

The boat pulled up to the dock and the captain expertly secured it with two ropes to posts. Father Lucian was the first to step out. He leaned back over the edge of the boat and offered a hand to Sarah to help her out. She took it and stepped over the edge. When her foot hit the dock, the island exploded into activity with hundreds of birds leaping from the trees in a thunderous sound of flapping. Then the bell sounded.

# 4

Father Lucian spun around and looked up at the bell tower. Sarah felt her eyes drawn to it. Not from the sound that just bonged from the distant tower. It was something more. Something more primal in her. An urge from deep within that accompanied the tingling that covered her entire body. The sensation was normally isolated to her back and neck. This came up through the ground entering the soles of her feet. It raced up her legs and shook her from the inside, all the way up to her head. The vibration called to her, spoke to her. Hundreds of thousands of beings, all trying to communicate at once.

"What is this place?", she asked with both feet firmly on the ground.

The captain replied, "Morte."

Sarah took several curious steps up the path toward the closest structure, a red brick building with white-trimmed windows and doors. The exterior was weathered and worn with cracks and signs of decay everywhere. Weeds and various forms of vegetation had made their home in the crevices of the walkway and every crack in the exterior walls. Portions of the exterior had fallen away from the structure. The decay continued as the structure transitioned from a single story building to a two story building that resembled a hospital. The two story building appeared to have nine rooms on each floor. It was an assumption that Sarah made based on the presence of nine windows lining the outside wall of each floor. None of which had glass. Then she considered the possibility that a central hall bisected each floor, making it eighteen rooms. After the ninth window, the building became three stories. There were eleven windows on each of those floors leading to the last structure connected to the building, the bell tower that stood watch over the boat dock, the structure below it, and its inhabitants, that Sarah felt. To her, every room in the place had a patient, and they were in pain. Physically, emotionally, and spiritually.

She turned back to her party. Father Lucian had helped both Sister Francesca and Sister Ester out of the boat and onto the dock. Both still prayed, but were wide-eyed taking in the scene with a hint of a quiver in their lips. It was fear. An emotion she hadn't seen from them before. Not even when faced with what Sarah carried on day-to-day. They followed Father Lucian closely, closer than they ever followed Sarah. If the sun were bright enough to cast a shadow, they would be his.

"Welcome to the Island of Poveglia," Father Lucian said. His voice trailed off and lacked the quiet confidence Sarah had come to know. "Its called the most haunted place on the face of the planet."

"And you brought me here?", Sarah asked, surprised.

"Yes. I want your thoughts, your help."

"Do you really think this is smart?", she asked. Her voice forceful and almost pleading. She felt the presence in the place. The screams were getting louder and heavier. She turned back toward the buildings a few times to try to convince herself there was nothing there, just broken old buildings that were decaying under the pressure of the sea and weather. Instead, she saw the building as it might have been when it was open. Shadows and figures moved in and out the windows. They looked at her, begging for her to help. Against what, she didn't know. "We need to leave, before I lose control."

The two sisters flinched, but Father Lucian stood steadfast and asked, "Sarah, are you feeling him?"

"No, but what I feel around us will draw him out." She paused and rubbed her eyes and then her face. Her hands attempted to scrub away what she felt and saw, but it was to no avail. Everything was still there.

"Was this some kind of prison?", asked Sarah, but before Father Lucian could answer, she gave her question a second thought. There were no guard towers. One might not think you would need one on an Island, but even Alcatraz had them. To her, this was the only option with what she felt. The pain, agony, and despair. Trapped on this island behind bars, with no hope to ever be free again. Destined to spend the rest of your life looking across the lagoon and seeing life go on in Venice, but never able to leave. Then her eyes searched the structure again. There were no bars. This wasn't a prison. It was a hospital. She corrected her question, "What kind of hospital was this?"

"Bravo Sarah. What told you it was a hospital?"

"The lack of bars. I first thought it was a prison, but there are no bars on the doors and windows."

"Well, that is an expert use of your deductive reasoning, but what do you feel? What does that tell you?"

Sarah took a few more steps toward a large white coped door that she assumed was some sort of main entrance. "Agony and despair are overwhelming, but there is something evil over the top of everything, like a blanket trapping and holding it all down. Something horrible happened here, didn't it?"

"Yes, it did. Sarah, this Island has been used for many purposes. Its history is speckled with horrific events, and some that are less horrific." Father Lucian walked away from Sarah, along the long wall of the building toward the two-story section. His hands pointed to the structure like a tour guide. His shadows had left him and became Sarah's shadow. "It was first settled about 1700 years ago by people fleeing barbaric rulers that beat and tortured them. Then it became a fortress to protect the Lagoon. This building is all that is left of the original structure. Its history took a turn in the late 1700s, when the office of Public Health turned it into a quarantine station for everyone, or everything, that entered the port. When the plague hit years after that, this island was the final destination for hundreds of thousands of those who suffered and died because of the horrible disease. Their bodies never left this place, neither did most of their souls. In the 20s they turned it into an asylum for the mentally ill, where a doctor took his job to the extremes and performed experimental surgeries on the patients until he went crazy himself and jumped out of the bell tower." Father Lucian pointed up at the tower that gonged when Sarah set foot on the island.

"Well Father, that is a totally terrorizing story, but it still doesn't explain why I am here."

"The legend says the dead, including the doctor, still roam the building."

Sarah didn't want to admit that she already knew that. Each time she looked at one of the structures, she swore she saw a shadow or presence move. It could have just been her eyes playing tricks on her in the fog, all triggered by what she felt, but she heavily doubted that. "So, you want me to confirm the legend or something?"

"No, the Church is not interested in legends of that sort. We do get involved when one of the living suffers at the hand of such a presence." He walked back toward the entrance where Sarah stood. The lines in his distinguished face took a downward turn. "Three weeks ago, two teenagers set off in a boat to do some fishing. The story they told the authorities is they heard someone crying for help so they approached the island, but never stepped foot on it. The screaming and cries continued, and they rode around the shore calling out for whoever it was. That was when, out of nowhere, something knocked both of them out of the boat and then turned it over. One came up immediately, but the other was pulled under repeatedly by something. That boy finally made it to the shore, but was then dragged off into the brush. His friend turned the boat back over and followed. He found him several minutes later, torn to shreds. That child is still in the hospital recovering. His friend suffered several scratches on his back as he pulled his friend out. The whole time, the screams for help continued and figures ran around them. Now, some may dismiss this as some sort of animal, but there is nothing over here. Others will look at the story and think it is something the young boys made up to cover for doing something they shouldn't have been doing when they got hurt, but I will tell you I visited both in the hospital at the request of my superiors. What I saw convinced me we needed to check it out. That is why you are here."

# 5

"So what do you expect to find?", Sarah asked.

"Unknown. I don't doubt there are spectral presences here, but hopefully that is all we find, and everyone was right about the boys' story."

Sarah stepped in through the main entrance first. The conditions inside didn't match what she saw on the outside. The cracked bricks and weathered facade were a stark contrast to the pristine, almost clinical appearance of the inside. Its plain white-tiled floors and white walls were shockingly immaculate. Not a spot of dust anywhere. No smudges on the wall or any signs of water damage, which was odd considering how open it was to the elements. The air inside smelled clean, clear, not musky or old. Her eyes caught a glint from one window and noticed something she hadn't from the outside. There was glass in the windows.

"Well, that explains it," she thought to herself. She looked through them again and wondered how she had looked right past them earlier. Each were remarkably clean, but they had little droplets of mist rolling down the outsides of them.

The others followed her inside as she moved to the center of the room. None of the others seemed to share their amazement at the state of the interior, but then again they were familiar with this place and knew of it. Maybe this was a common fact that everyone was aware of. The Office of Public Health must still take steps to keep it clean for some reason. All valid possibilities she could consider, but none were the great mystery of why she had been brought here. To refocus herself on the task, she began to ask Father Lucian where they needed to go to next, but then she felt something pull to her. Something further inside, and she continued through a door and across a threshold into the next building.

"Ah ha," she was right. Just as she thought, a central hallway bisected the floors of the two story structure. Doors line the walls on each side of the hallway. They opened up to rooms with one window each. There was no doubting this was part of the hospital, not with how this was laid out. She walked past the first doors, but then stopped at the second and looked into the one on the right. Like the hallway, it was clean, if that was a strong enough word to describe its condition. Inside, a small stainless steel table and pole on a dolly sat positioned neatly next to a bed which was still made with white linens, with hospital corners of course. She raced across the hall to the opposing door and peered inside. The room was an exact copy of the one she'd just left. As were the next two. All sat and waited for patients to arrive.

She stepped inside the next one and walked around the bed. Above her, a fluorescent light hummed. She hadn't noticed power before, but was not surprised to see it on. Keeping the lights on probably deterred unwanted visitors and helped the Policia if they stop by on any regular patrols. The bed in that room became her new focus of fascination. The linens on the bed were not only white, they were an unnatural bleached, almost eye-hurting white. Little lines of shadows told her where the creases were still stuck in the fabric's memory from the last time they had been folded. She had seen that many times before, but not in quite a while. Her mother always rotated sheets. When she took one set off a bed to wash, she had another in a closet ready to put back on. The creases were visible for a few hours until the fabric finally relaxed.

She continued to walk down the hall, which was more of the same until she reached the far corner. Unlike the rest of the floor, it wasn't a room. Just a counter with a chair behind it. She ran her finger along the top of the countertop as she walked down its length. It was cool to the touch, and clean. Her eyes watched the chair as she passed it. It appeared to swivel and follow her, but she knew how crazy that thought sounded. Was it just her eyes playing a trick on her, or something else? That something that made the entire island vibrate. The same something that that pulled her toward the stairs and up to check out the second floor, which she ascended and entered without hesitation.

It was a carbon copy of the first floor. nine rooms on one side, eight on the other, with a nurses station at one end. The chair was in the same spot relative to the counter as it was on the first floor, and just like on the first floor, it appeared to swivel to follow her as she walked by. There was even a little squeak that caused her to look back at it after she had fully passed by. It wasn't moving at that time. She entered the area and walked around the chair. An old rotary phone sat on the desk behind the counter with several upright racks next to it to hold folders. She bent down and pulled open one drawer, not sure what she expected to find. Gloves? Syringes? Neither. Paper. A pre-printed paper form on clean white paper. There were stacks of the form sitting there, with a box of old ball-point pens next to them just waiting to be used to fill one out. Her fingers ran along the edge of the paper and fanned the stack ever so slightly. It brought a smile to her face. Why it amused her, here and now, was a complete mystery to her. She did it again, and again. Enjoying the sound it made, which was almost a little rip as the edges brushed against her fingertips as they fell back into place. Once more she did it and let out a little giggle that echoed through the empty hall. The sound of her voice didn't startle her. The sound of leather-soled shoes slapping on the tile coming in her direction did.

Sarah jerked up from the drawer and let it slam shut with a bang. The footfalls stopped before she leaned across the counter to look down the hall. Feeling somewhat silly, she remembered there were three others in the building besides her. What she saw, or didn't see, removed that feeling and replaced it with terror. No one was there. No Father Lucian. No Sister Francesca or Sister Esther. Sarah panicked. Her breath quickened to just short of hyperventilation. Her hand grabbed hold of the counter and slung her body around it and back into the hallway. The shoes she wore temporarily lost their grip on the glossy tile, sending her sliding. When she regained control, she rushed back down the stairs. At the bottom she looked out, and they weren't there either. *"Where were they?"* was the only thought in the front of her mind, while the back of it was clouded with fear that their absence opened her up to Abaddon coming forward and taking control of her again.

"What was that prayer?", she muttered to herself while standing in the door of the stairs. She scanned up and down the hallway for the three others, who had vanished.

"What was it?", she said out loud again. Mother Demiana never told her what the prayer was. Sarah had asked a few times for her to tell her, just in case of an emergency when she might find herself alone, like this very moment. Each time her holy Mother told her it would not work that way. She would not be able to use the prayer to contain him. Someone else has to be the one that contains it. That was news that both disappointed and frightened Sarah, but, like Father Lucian had also told her, Mother Demiana told her that in time she would learn how to control it herself; just not with a prayer.

"Father!", she called. Her voice echoing down the long hall. There was no response.

"Sisters!"

Still hearing nothing but silence, her worry grew and her pulse quickened. She rushed down the hall, repeating her "Our Father" and "Hail Mary" with each gasp of air she took as she ran to the main entrance and out the door. Outside again, the fog was thicker, the buildings and the dock were clearly in view. The boat wasn't. It was gone.

A thought flashed in her head, but she knew there was no way Father Lucian would have left her there. Or had he? Had she become so dangerous that they abandoned her on this island? That had to be it. She had had no issues since she'd arrived at the Abbey, or had she? Maybe she wasn't even aware of it when it happened. She had become too strong and too difficult for the sisters to maintain control over. She remembered the tone in Mother Demiana's voice when she heard them talking. The worry and concern. Was she talking to Father Lucian about her? Telling him how hard it was to control her? Or maybe it was her reaction to Father Lucian's plan to trap Sarah on this Island alone.

"These were people of God, how could they desert me here?" she wondered out loud. Sarah searched the fog for the boat through the single tear that ran down her cheek. She sat down and took the black veil off of her head and sat holding it in her lap. First her body shuddered, then slowly tear by tear she began to wail. Around her the fog thickened, and the despair set in with a weight that pushed her further down the hole she had started descending.

From inside that dark void, she wondered about her future. Were there people here to tend to her needs? Would anyone come back to bring food? Surely, they didn't intend for her to sit here and starve to death. Alas, she didn't have the answers to those questions. One overriding detail remained and overshadowed every possible positive answer. She shared an existence with a very dangerous being. One that threatened the existence of life itself. Her life is just one life. Could they be sacrificing one life for the safety of everyone else?

The thought sank in, and her head dropped a little lower. Her tears rolled a little stronger down her cheeks. She wailed a little louder as her hands balled up the black veil and squeezed it with all her might. Then she heard a giggle come from the main entrance. Her head spun around and saw lights shining through every window of the complex.

# 6

The world behind her that had seemed dead, now appeared to breathe with life. Lights and sounds filled the landscape. Both drove the despair from her thoughts, opening room for more fear to move in. Sarah was never a person who was driven by fear before what happened in Miller's Crossing. Where most people would run if they saw the sight she did, or heard that odd giggle that seemed to come from the building itself, she wouldn't. She would feel a wondrous curiosity that drew her toward such places. That changed after what happened, not because she was afraid for what she saw or heard, but because she was afraid of what was in her.

She stood up, both hands still giving her black veil a working over to release the nerves. The fog had become dense, almost a steady mist that gave the glow of the lights a mystical appearance. Another glance up and down the dock confirmed that she was still alone, but that didn't stop one more attempt to call out, "Father Lucian, where are you? Sisters?"

The only reply was the same eerie giggle which came from the building with a muffled crash. It sounded like a metal tray or object had been dropped somewhere deep inside the structure. Someone was there and, without thinking, Sarah went in to find them.

Once again she entered the main entrance. The florescent lights buzzed above her, and the entire world still vibrated around her, just like it had when she first stepped on shore. There was something else there now, a hum. Like a crowded theatre just before a movie, with hundreds of conversations all taking place at the same time. The volume ebbed up and down, with spikes here and there, but it remained a single sound. She couldn't discern any voices from one another, nor could she hear any words, just the hum.

Both the hum and vibration increased in intensity and volume the further she walked in. Occasionally, she heard something moving, or something falling. A cart on wheels rolled down the hall behind her. Footsteps behind her, in front, and beside her. They stepped in and out of rooms, down the hallway, into the nurses' station, where Sarah had now paused to stand and listen. The chair was still there, as was the phone, which she'd heard ring twice in the hum. Ahead of her, steps echoed in the stairwell, going both up and down the stairs. Those that came down continued once they reached the ground floor and either turned and went to the next building or turned and came past her. A few times, she felt a slight chill in her arms when they passed, forcing goosflesh on both aarms and up her neck.

Minutes had passed since she last heard the giggle or the crash and unsure where to go she continued deeper down the hallway of the first story, beyond the bell tower, and around the corner, to an outside hallway. She stepped outside into a silent world curtained in a dense fog. To her left, was just shadows of overgrown bushes and weeds. They looked like great beasts that stood guard over the island and leaned ominously toward her. To her right was the fractured exterior of another building which unlike the others had three steps that led up to two large wooden doors. The steps had seen better days, with cracks running through the stones and large chunks missing from both them and the ornate stone railing that funneled you up to the doors. Large iron rings served as handles for the doors. Each pitted and corroded from years of exposure. She grabbed hold of both, then looked at the hinges on the outside. They were large corroded pieces of flat iron, much like you would see on a barn door. She found it odd. They were on the outside instead of inside, and gave the rings a pull, but they didn't open. Then she gave them a push.

They opened easily, and a brisk breeze of stale air rushed out and passed her as both arms held the weighty doors open. This added to the chill her body already felt thanks to the vibration and presence of whatever was here. Inside was a simple stone chapel. Complete with two rows of pews, a simple wooden altar, and a cross at the front. Her gaze scanned the walls and floor of the familiar and comforting setting. She felt safe here and moved to the altar to say a quick prayer for her safety and protection. The heels of her shoes clicked on the cobble stone floor. It provided an uneven surface to walk on, forcing her to look down and watch each step. Her movement stopped short of a line of red cobbles. It went from wall to wall and was a few feet short of the altar itself. Nothing in particular told her the significance of the line, but she didn't want to chance a misstep so she crossed herself and knelt right there.

Sarah prayed for her safety and, before she stood up, remembering the story Father Lucian told her about the island, she said a prayer for the souls of those who'd died here. When she completed that prayer and said, "Amen", that same cool brisk breeze that blew past her when she opened the door, now rushed back into the chapel blowing her forward. She caught herself with her hands on the cobbles just before she landed on the other side of the red line and hurried to her feet. Behind her the two large wooden doors shut with a thunderous slam, sending her into a brief moment of darkness. Candles soon illuminated the chapel from all sides. Sarah spun to her right and watched a bank of votive candles flicker to life. The bank on the other side of the room was already lit. Each and every candle. Two large candles on tall holders flanked either side of the altar.

A voice emerged from behind the altar. It was speaking Italian, very fast and loaded with passion. It had a sing-song tone that she recognized almost instantly. It was a priest giving a sermon.

She shuffled her feet backwards on the floor, toward the doors. Past the rows of pews. Her gaze scanned back and forth between the votives on either side of the room and the altar, and back again. There was no movement besides the dancing of the candle flames. Her hand reached behind her to feel for the door, but grasped only air. A few more steps and another try, still air. After another step, she finally felt it, and searched for a handle, but found none. She spun around to look with her eyes, and there was nothing on this side of the doors. No handle. No hinges. Just flat dark wooden planks that stood vertically to make up the door. This drove her panic deeper, with the faint thought that this was not a real chapel, but something Abaddon had created in her mind to trap her.

Sarah continued to search with her hands for anything to grip, but the planks were flat and smooth. The gap between the two doors was large enough to feel air moving through, but too small for her to wiggle a finger into. That didn't stop her from frantically clawing at the gap to gain some kind of leverage to open the door. Behind her, the priest continued his impassioned sermon. She didn't bother trying to hear what he said. She heard the passion in his voice, but didn't care. She wanted out of there, if that was even possible. Each failed attempt to move the doors ratcheted up her panic. She wouldn't let Abaddon win this time. She couldn't. Even though she still didn't know how to control him on her own. This all had to be his doing. In each of these panic-fueled thoughts, was weaved the harsh reality that those she trusted brought her and left her here in this evil place, left her here to die.

The sermon continued, but having been through enough of them, she could tell he was reaching his climax just based on his tone. What was next? Again, she had no intention of being there to find out. She hoped she still had the choice, the capability to get out. Then, a painful moment of hope. The nail on her right index finger caught the grain in the gap between the two doors for the briefest of moments. The door inched in before closing again. The sermon behind her had reached a fevered pitch. She clawed at the door again with both hands. Two nails on her left hand snapped off completely to the quick, and she shrieked in pain and held her damaged fingers tightly in her other hand. Tears streamed down her face. Her right hand continued to claw at the now bloodstained wood, to gain any hold on the door. A small splinter gave way on the door and jammed itself under her fingernail and into her tender skin, producing another scream of pain that echoed in the chamber. The priest behind her was yelling now, at the top of his lungs, and then stopped.

Hundreds of voices commanded, "Grazie a Dio," behind her, and then the doors exploded open, knocking Sarah backward and onto both of her injured hands. She scrambled to her feet and rushed out through the doors as fast as she could in a directionless sprint. Both hands held close to her body.

# 7

She ran through the weeds and brushes. The thorn-covered vines cut through her habit and sliced her arms. When she stopped, she was surrounded by a briar's patch of pain. Anywhere she could go, she would have to push through the vines and suffer more violations of her flesh by the thorns. The buildings were nowhere to be seen. Not even the glow of the lights in the fog. She didn't remember the direction she came from. When she bolted out of the Chapel, she ran blindly into the brush. She remembered making several turns to avoid trees and thicker sections of thickets, but was unsure where those were. Behind her, which would be the obvious selection to backtrack, the weeds had already filled in and removed any evidence she had moved through the area. Any attempt to backtrack would be merely a path of guesses.

Sarah spun around and suffered additional cuts to her shoulders. Her gaze searched for any sign, any evidence of the best way to go. In the fog and the shadows, she appeared to be surrounded, with only a small break in the towering foliage ahead of her. That opening wasn't there a moment ago, and inside she felt something pull her in that direction, the spine-tingling sensation that, for just a moment, emerged above the constant vibration and chill of this place. Even the fog seemed less dense in that direction.

With no other options, she took one step forward. A thorn tore into her shoulder again, but the sensation, the pull toward that direction increased. Another step, and another rip of her flesh. This one was deep, and she felt drops of warm fluid run down her shoulder. She whimpered and reached up with her other hand to wipe the wound. It came away covered with smeared blood, producing another whimper from her, but that sound was nothing compared to the scream that came from in front of her. Beads of cold sweat developed on her forehead and a slight tremble progressed down Sarah's arms to her hands.

With no way to turn back, she pushed forward, and suffered several more cuts until she found herself out on a worn path. It was nothing more than a bare path in the grass. The weeds and brush that dominated the open areas of the island were not here, as if their growth pattern had been trained through years and decades of travel. The ground had a rut, a small groove in it that was too small to be from foot traffic, unless someone walked the path in careful steps from heel to toe, one foot after another.

In both directions the path led into the dense fog, with no clue of what lay at the end, but her instincts and another screech that curdled her blood and made her gasp, told her she needed to go to the right. A direction she moved slowly, cautiously. The vibration she felt when she stepped off the boat increased, and became all-inclusive. As was the cold chill that progressed up and down her body in waves. Each increasing in frequency and intensity.

The path took Sarah to a simple white-railed bridge that connected the main island to a smaller one. Drops of mist puddled on the top of the railing. Their surface in constant motion, with ripples moving in and out in all directions. Sarah walked up the incline of the arched bridge. Each step an investigation. She stopped, looked, and felt before the next step. At the top, she paused longer than she had to that point. The sensations were stronger, but her eyes told her the island was just another overgrown patch of land, with weeds and vines everywhere. Still, there was something that pulled her further, closer, and she followed that instinct and proceeded down to the other side.

Sarah was not prepared for what happened when she stepped off the bridge on the other side. The world she had seen peeled away and exposed the fire and brimstone version of hell on Earth. She was surrounded by every feeling and facet of death. Souls moaned and howled. Bodies lay open on top of the ground, some smoldered and turned to dust right in front of her. Each turned their head to look deep into her gaze as the flames moved up and over them. The wind blew the last embers of burning dust away. Others lay unburnt, while birds picked and pulled at their flesh. Some dead, an obvious state confirmed by the stench she smelled, but others were not. They swung arms, that were nothing more than bones draped with flesh, at the birds, which pushed them away for only a second before they returned. They screamed as chunks of flesh were ripped from their bodies.

The screams were no longer a mournful one; it was one that was more horrifying to her, more personal. "Sister, help me!", they pleaded. Hundreds of sets of eyes all trained on her.

"Sister, help me!" they yelped in unison. The same gaunt and decaying arms that battled the birds were now reaching out toward her.

All their pain and suffering flooded into and overwhelmed Sarah, knocking her to her knees. Clouds of fine dust rose up from the impact. The dust hovered around her and swirled, suffocating her, until it cleared above her head.

Sarah gasped for breath and fell to her hands, which produced two more clouds of dust. She coughed, gagged, and wheezed. All the while, her body felt the horrifying outflowing of terror and dread channel through her. She held both eyes tightly closed, to protect against the dust and the sights around her.

One voice broke free from the "Sister, help me!" chorus, and pleaded, "No. No. Let me go." It was the scratchy voice of a man. Elderly or sick, if she attempted to make a guess based on how weak it sounded. It pleaded again, and this time they sounded closer. Sarah felt an impulse to open her eyes, but she resisted it. She squeezed them closed and ignored the icy fingers of fear that tightened their grip on her soul.

The voice pleaded again, this time closer, and it was not alone. A squeak of an ungreased wheel rolled toward her. "Help me, Sister. Stop him."

Sarah still wouldn't open her eyes. She crossed herself quickly, almost failing to complete the shape of the cross before her right hand stopped and joined her left in prayer. She prayed every prayer she knew. All the "Our Father" and "Hail Mary" prayers she could utter were mixed in with the Lord's Prayer. The squeak and pleas came closer still. Other voices then joined his plea, "Sister, help him."

The squeak and the pleading man were now close enough for her to tell where they were. They were close, and coming toward her from her left. In between squeaks, she thought she could hear footsteps on the ground. They thudded down and crunched the dust beneath them. She continued to pray, faster now. Having run out of the traditional prayers, she resorted back to those she had used before. Some that were written by her family in the book, others that she made up on the spot based on her own training. She tried anything, but nothing worked. At no time did the sounds go away. At no time did she feel the power of her faith build up inside her. She didn't stop though. Each time she moved on to the next, desperate to find something that worked.

"Sister, please!", screamed the voice, just feet from her ears. The wheel squeaked past her and up the wooden bridge. The footsteps pounded the bridge like cannon shots. The ground shook under her.

"Sister!", it screeched, now behind her. The voice dripped with pain and death. Each syllable, especially the second, drawn out, wanting and haunting, clawed at her essence and threatened to pull her very life from her.

"There's no helping him, Sister. Just go on praying," demanded an evil voice.

# 8

Once the shivers left Sarah, she found the courage to open her eyes and stand up. Before her, the island was alive. Bodies on death's doorstep all reached for her, called for her. Eyes of black coal, that took on a silver glow in the eerie glow, stared right through her. The voices of the chorus became more of a shrill shriek, dissolving the words they had uttered for help and salvation into a single haunting sound that never stopped.

As chilling as that scene was, it was not what sent the shivers up and down her being. That was what was behind her, rolling away further with every passing moment. She let them get a little further over the bridge and down the path before turning around. Even then, it was a slow and reluctant turn. She had hoped her gaze wouldn't see anything more than the fog. With as thick as it was, there was little doubt whatever it was had disappeared into the bank by now. What she saw dissolved that hope. The orange glow of a lantern swung in the grey. Sarah followed.

Keeping her distance, Sarah walked behind the lantern and retraced the path she'd taken to the bridge, and then finding a new one back to the complex of buildings. The whole way she heard the squeak of the wheel of whatever it, he, or whatever it was pushing was. More ghastly than the squeak was the constant scream for help. The man continued to call to her, "Sister! Stop him! Help me!"

Sarah continued to follow, and even eased closer to get a better look. Her gaze and mind on what was there in front of her. Then her body all but jumped, as she heard the loud snap of a single stick that cracked beneath the weight of her left foot. Both hands yanked up to cover her mouth, but the gasp still escaped. Her eyes exploded open and stared forward. Everything in her expected the lantern to stop and come back toward her. The tremble she felt earlier started again, causing the stick and the dust-like gravel under her feet to rustle and crunch. She could hear it. It was the loudest sound on the whole island. Whatever she was following had to hear it, too. What would happen when they came back?

*Come on, Sarah,* she thought to herself. *You are tougher than this. Nothing has ever scared you before.* She reminded herself several times she is one of only a handful of people trained to deal with all this. That was assuming this was paranormal.

She reached around her neck for her chain and pulled up the crucifix Mother Demiana  put around her neck when she first met her in Miller's Crossing. No, it wasn't made from the wood of the cross Christ was crucified on, but it would have to do. She gave it a kiss and then took the chain off her neck and held it out, once again reciting the prayers. Her stare looked past the cross at the lantern. It hadn't paused. It hadn't turned. It continued on. The destination was unknown, but Sarah was determined to find out, and she once again followed. Each step, now taken with more care than she had before.

Through a jungle of weeds and brushes that towered over her head, she kept on the narrow path. The rut in the grass and ground she'd noticed before made more sense now that she heard the squeak of a wheel. Both facts fed her already overactive imagination. For there to be a single rut, it had to just be one wheel. That made sense. She had only heard one squeak. The image of some ghastly creature pushing a single-wheeled wheelbarrow popped into her mind. The decimated and decaying body of the man who screamed for her lain across it like some game scored on a hunt.

This imagination had always played with her mind when she was out dealing with issues of the spectral kind. In most instances, it forced her to imagine things that were worse than they were. Instead of a single translucent figure floating in a field, her mind spent the drive to wherever it was, running through an array of ghosts and hordes of other creatures standing there waiting to attack her. Most of the time, it was some kind of image of a zombie, something she credited to the amount of movies on that subject she'd watched growing up. She could blame Hollywood. During her impressionable teenage years, if it didn't have a zombie in it, then it didn't sell, so everything leaned that way. Everything from blockbusters, to shows, and even books. A few even appeared to be forced. Almost as if the producers or agencies approached the writer and said something like, "This is a great story, but can you add a zombie into it? They sell." Only a few times did reality ever match or exceed the worst her imagination dug up. As the shadow of what she followed took shape against the emerging glow of the lights from the old buildings, she hoped this was another one of those cases.

It was a man, no mythical creature or beast from a nightmare with arms and claws that dangled down. Not particularly tall or hulking, just a man in a long coat. As the lantern swung closer to him, she could see the coat was white. The lantern which she thought hung from his hand, hung from one of the handles of the object he pushed. It swung back and forth, at times giving her more of a view of him, and others giving more of a view of the brushes, vine, and thickets the path wove through. Their destination was no longer a mystery to Sarah. The old hospital was the only structure on that end of the island.

As they came closer, her belief of where this journey would end became more definitive. There was something new. A sound that wasn't here the last time. The closer they came, the clearer the sound was. For the second time in the last several minutes she heard voices, but these didn't call out to her. It was the sound of hundreds of people. Some screaming, some having conversations. None she could hear specifically, but the differences in tone and tenor of each were undeniable. There were people here, or what used to be people.

This was something Sarah had experienced many times. It was quite common to hear conversations between paranormal visitors. They are the most common reported characteristic for every reported haunting in the world. What people heard, when they really heard something and didn't just fall prey to their mind or others, were either real conversations, or echoes from the past. At the moment, she didn't know which she heard. She rarely ever found out for sure.

The sound grew, and the conversations became more discernible. Several female voices spoke calmly, in Italian of course, as weak and pained male voices exclaimed and yelled several of the Italian swear words she had taught herself via the internet on her first visit to the Vatican. Objects moved. Doors slammed.

The man with a lantern approached the back entrance to the three story section. He stopped at the door and walked up to it, leaned in, and yelled something. Sarah had a full view of the object he pushed. Her hopes were dashed. This wasn't one of those cases. What she saw matched what she had imagined and her gaze rested on the man splayed across the wheelbarrow for but a second. Two men in white uniforms, orderlies, came out through the door with a gurney. Together, they lifted the man off of the wheelbarrow. He screamed and hung onto the edge of it as if his life depended on it. When his grip slipped, he kicked and punched all the way to the gurney. Neither orderly showed any ill effects of the few random swings that landed squarely against them. The man was weak, and near death, but he still used what strength he had left to fight until he was laid down and secured with straps. His head bucked back and forth, slamming into the padded surface as the only protest he had left.

The gurney and orderlies disappeared through the doorway. The man, who Sarah could now see wore a long white lab coat, followed them closely.

Sarah, intrigued more than frightened, and still unsure if what she was seeing was something real, or a creation of the demon inside her, to distract. Even though her hunch said it was more likely the latter, she wanted to follow, but waited several moments before slipping her crucifix back over her head and stepping up to the door.

The peeling paint and mold stains that had adorned the door before were gone. Her hand reached and gave a slight shove on the clean and freshly-painted yellow door. It opened without even the softest grind in the hinges. She stepped inside the building for the third time that day, but this time she entered a world that was unlike any she had experienced before. The floor was active. Patients called for nurses from their rooms. Nurses in white uniforms with skirts that stopped at the knees and white pill hats balanced on their nicely kept hair, rushed around from the station to the rooms with assortments of charts and cups. Doctors, who looked as if they were fresh out of med school, were in tow behind them, going from room to room. One paused in the middle of the hall and looked at Sarah. Not past her or through her, as many spirits did, but at her. The man, no older than her, with black-rimmed glasses, and dark hair that hadn't seen a comb in several days, which by the look of his eyes and the rest of him, was probably the last time he'd slept, nodded at her and then continued into the room. Beyond him was the back of the doctor's white coat as he followed the two orderlies down the hall.

# 9

These weren't spirits. Or not ones she was used to. They were flesh and blood, nothing translucent or haunting. A detail that, again, led her more to believe this was Abaddon's work. What she saw from where she stood in the hall resembled what you might see in any normal hospital, but this wasn't a normal hospital. Only half an hour ago, this was an abandoned building. Now it was full of the sick and dying, with doctors and nurses running around trying to soothe their patients with feeble attempts to prolong their life against death. Sarah remembered what Father Lucian had told her before he left, this was the island they brought those with the plague to die. There was something honorable, almost noble, in what Sarah saw. They must know that nothing they did would save their patients. This was a losing battle. The big question in her mind, when one nurse bumped into her: Why was she seeing it?

She didn't have an answer, and wasn't sure this is where one would be found. Perhaps the answer lay with that man she'd followed in from the field. When she had stopped, he had stopped and waited on her. She dodged nurses and doctors as she followed him down the hallway. A few times she peered into an open door she passed. Inside, a moaning and coughing patient now occupied the neatly made bed with clean white sheets she'd seen earlier. Blood spittle sprayed out on the sheet with every breath. Others lay silently with long tubes running from under large bandaged areas of their bodies and into reservoirs that hung on the side of their beds. Some were filled with red fluid. Others with something that looked like a black sludge.

Each time she looked back down the hallway, the procession of the doctor and two orderlies had paused, as if to wait on her, yet again. When she started, they started. She followed, still looking, but never pausing at the rooms. They crossed over into the building that was only two stories and entered the first room on the left. Sarah slowed to a creep and approached the door. She looked inside from the edge of the doorway. This room was different from the others, and one she hadn't noticed before. It was larger than the others, or appeared that way. Missing were the hospital bed and steel table and racks. In their place were large lights hanging from the ceiling, and tables along the walls. A quick glance at the scalpels, bone saws, stainless spreaders, and other assorted surgical devices told her exactly what this was. It was an operating room. Of course, there would be one in the building, this was a hospital, she thought to herself, and eased up on her caution allowing herself to step further into the doorway. The man on the gurney continued to strain against the straps. His gurney was now situated directly in the center of the room, under the lights. Both orderlies stood with the doctor at the sink, washing up. The man on the gurney saw her during one of his attempts to pull up against the straps. His hand jerked and reached in her direction. "Sister! Save me. Stop them before they kill me," he exclaimed.

Sarah stumbled backward, crashing into the open door with a thud. She turned to run out.

"Sister, don't mind him. He is delirious with fever. You can't save him. Nobody can, really, but I am going to try." The doctor looked over his shoulder at her. His body remained in motion, carefully scrubbing his hands. "I have been battling this disease for close to twenty years now. Traditional means have never worked. I believe surgical might be the secret."

He finished and turned. Both hands held up and out. An orderly, a tall redheaded man with broad shoulders who looked like he belonged more in a prison guard uniform than a set of white scrubs, picked up a pair of gloves from the table and delicately maneuvered them onto the doctor's hands. The doctor made a few final adjustments to his gloves before he stepped to the gurney. The hulking redhead put on his own pair of gloves, while the second orderly, a sandy-blonde with dark beady eyes and an uneven smile that gave him a slightly maniacal appearance, gathered the scalpel and several other medical instruments on a tray and walked over, placing them next to their patient on the gurney. He stood by the tray, with his eyes fixed on the doctor, who looked the patient from head to toe, over and over again.

The doctor took one long latex-covered finger and slowly traced a line along the man's ribcage and up to his throat. With his finger still finishing the top of the line along the collar bone, he held his other hand out flat. In an instant, a scalpel was placed in the palm, and his fingers closed around it. Sarah watched as the point glistened in the surgical lights as it moved to join his finger up by the collar bone. It hovered above the man's flesh for just a mere second before the edge made a slow insertion and slice. It had moved less than half an inch when the man on the gurney shrieked and threw all four extremities as far as the straps would allow.

"Raul!" shouted the doctor. The sandy-blonde beast in white moved to the patient's head and restrained him while the scalpel cut further. The shriek continued, and the man's toes and fingers reached out as far as their joints would allow. His body became rigid while the sound continued to flow from his mouth. Seemingly impervious to what was going on around him, the doctor continued to retrace the line, this time with a scalpel in a steady hand, and not his finger. The cut continued down the man's sternum. Blood oozed up and pooled on his sunken in chest. No attempt was made by either orderly or doctor to soak it up with any of the sponges or gauze that remained on the table against the wall. The image and the smell made Sarah's stomach do somersaults, prompting a quick swallow to keep it from coming up in protest.

The shrieks had died down, or the man had passed out from the pain, when the doctor had finished the incision and placed the scalpel back on the tray. The fingers of both hands retraced the cut, starting from either end, meeting in the middle. His fingers probed under the incision's edges. The skin pulled a bit. With a mighty yank, the doctor pulled the skin away from the man's muscle and bones by several inches. Whether the patient was awake or passed out before, there was no doubt he was awake now. His body jerked and heaved while his mouth shrieked. Sarah let one of her own out at the gruesome sight of a man being skinned alive.

"Why wasn't he given any anesthesia?" she roared in between shrieks. Her lips and jaw trembled, and both hands were extended straight down at her side, raising and jerking down to emphasize every word.

The doctor was the picture of calm as he turned toward her. Blood dripped from his gloves and landed on the floor with faint plops. "Sister. I need him awake to find the disease. Only when the symptoms are gone, do I know I have removed it."

He turned and ripped at the skin again. It held firm, at first, then gave way with a moist tear. Splatters of blood flew everywhere, and Sarah swallowed several more times to hold her stomach down. Her hands were positioned over her mouth. just in case, also to stifle another scream. Her body felt the waves of fear and sickness rolling inside and bent over instinctually.

The doctor reach into the bloody mass of tissue and bone and yanked on the man's rib cage. The first crack was all Sarah could take. This wasn't medicine. This was a massacre.

"You're a monster," she yelled.

The doctor froze. His head cocked to the side. When he turned around, the modest, unassuming forty-something doctor she saw before was not there anymore. This person was aggressive, and his eyes sloped up to an evil peak. Sharp and jagged teeth were visible in his gaping mouth as he seethed. "This is medicine. I am brave enough to try things no other doctor would to fight this. Just because you took an oath to God, don't believe you are someone who can stand in judgement of me."

Around her the room darkened and the clean and pristine operating room took on a dank and neglected appearance. Mold stains ran down the walls from the ceiling until they reached the floor and spread into larger stains. Holes appeared in the walls, and the fluorescent lights that hummed above flicked off, sending Sarah into both physical and spiritual darkness.

The doctor came toward her, his gloves still dripping the blood of the man onto the dirty and cracked floor. Her pulse quickened as she felt a level of evil within him above the pin pricks and sensations that covered the island. It was the same feeling she'd felt out in the field, as he'd passed. Her body still felt sick and tortured, but she managed to command it to run through the open door. She only made it two steps until she came to a halt in the center of the hallway where the world she'd entered was not the one she had left just moments earlier.

# 10

The hallway was a hall or terrors. Bodies, some mutilated and others half decomposed, lay on gurneys outside the rooms. Bodies in nurse's uniforms roamed around the hallways, bumping into walls and each other. They let out woeful moans with every step. Their trek had no direction, just a meander.

Sarah dodged the macabre medical professionals as she worked her way down the hall. Her body trembled and shook, but only slightly, and just from the initial shock. Adrenaline quickly flooded her body to force out the fear. This was a familiar world to Sarah. She had seen and experienced far worse through her years. The sight of decaying bodies did little to her. She had watched scenes of bodies decapitated, the human form torqued in the most unnatural ways, and grotesque distortions, as demons did their worst to their host, or put on a good show to break the will of the exorcist sent to deal with them.

"Stop her!" bellowed a voice from behind her. She turned to see the doctor, with the same jagged toothy grin. Behind him, the two hulking orderlies followed. Each now looked less human than before. Large jagged surgical scars ran across each of their faces. Large flaps of skin were missing, showing the bloody and pulsating tissue underneath. The flesh was missing on the left arm of the one the doctor had called Raul. Both pushed past the doctor and rushed after her. Any patients or nurses in their way were violently deposited in a heap of cracked bones and mangled bodies, against the closest walls.

Sarah picked up her pace, down the hallway, back toward the main entrance she had originally entered. A frequent gaze back confirmed they still followed her. Her first need was to get out of the building, but then where? She was on an island, with no way off. Based on her training, she knew some paranormal beings are tied to a particular place or structure. The attachment is usually something personal on an emotional or traumatic level. She hoped these two were tied to the building, and wouldn't be able to follow her out. Worst case would be if they were only attached to the island itself. That meant they could follow her out to the dock and anywhere else on the island. Then what? Could she swim for help? There were a few resorts on neighboring islands, but she had no idea how far away they were.

One thing at a time, she reminded herself while she continued to weave around wailing creatures in the hall. Similar screams came out of each of the rooms as she passed. Sarah only glanced into two of them as she passed. In one of them, the top half jerked and fought against the wires that suspended him from the ceiling. Only a mass of bloody bandage existed below the waist. Blood continued to cascade to the floor below him.

A man sat on his bed in the second room. He called for help. Help that would never come. Both hands removed, with just stumps at his wrists, and the entire right side of his scalp was missing, exposing his grey cranial matter. His gaze locked with Sarah's. His pain and grief overcame her and distracted her momentarily, but that was all it took for her to collide with a patient-loaded gurney being pushed out of a room by a nurse.

Sarah's body landed on the patient and then half bounced, half recoiled down to the floor. The blood from his skinless body smeared on her hands, face, and habit. He didn't scream from the impact, neither did Sarah. The nurse, with holes for eyes, chastised her carelessness, or so Sarah assumed. Her shouts were a rapid succession of Italian terms. They flooded at Sarah faster than she could understand. Not that she was too concerned with trying. Her mind was not on this collision, but on those that chased her. Without even looking back, she could sense they had gained significant ground.

A quick glance backward confirmed that, as Raul reached for her. She ducked barely in time. The bottom side of his meaty palm whacked her on the top of her head. The hallway tilted back and forth just before her vision blinked to black. When it came back into view, the world around her was muffled and spinning. The nurse continued to scream at her, but Sarah couldn't hear her. Nor could she really hear any of the random moans and cries. It was all a single buzzing roar. She felt a hand grip her shoulder. Without waiting to look at who it was, she used her other hand to knock it off and then attempted to stand. The gurney with the skinless patient still blocked her way, but she couldn't let that stop her, and pulled herself up onto it, with every intention of hurdling over it to flee down the hallway.

Her body had news for her. Everything spun again as she climbed up on the patient. She had to reach down with both hands and hold onto him to avoid falling to either side. Her stomach turned and her body twisted as she hung on. All the while he looked up at her, bright white eyes in a sea of oozing red tissue.

Raul's hand grabbed her right arm with a bone-crushing grip. That pain was all she needed to clear her head long enough to kick her leg against him. The impact pushed him backwards, but also knocked her over the gurney. She thought better of the move as she braced for impact with the tile floor. Her neck muscles tensed up, and she attempted to duck her head to protect against another impact. Her left side, shoulder, and hip took most of the brunt of it, which didn't feel too bad at first. It was a different story when she tried to stand. Pain shot through her hip and leg, forcing her back down to the ground.

Sarah heard a crash behind her and knew Raul had thrown the gurney and patient against the wall, as he had most of those he'd encountered in the hall. She tried to get up again, but it was no use. She couldn't even stand up, much less take a step, without the bolts of pain sending her back to the ground. A sense of foreboding evil grew inside her. It was a constant feeling while on the island, but there were times it grew more pronounced and closer to her. This time she knew why, and she knew what. The two large hands that grabbed both of her arms and yanked her up off the floor told her there was nothing she could do about it.

He slammed Sarah onto an empty gurney and strapped her down. She fought with every ounce of strength in her to break the straps but, much like the man she watched get rolled into the operating room, her attempts were futile. The leather straps gave a little with each yank, but returned the favor. Blood trickled from wounds on both wrists where the straps dug into and cut her skin. She felt the warm presence of blood on her ankles, too. She knew she couldn't beg for her release. The demonic face, with yellow eyes and a smile of yellowed and broken teeth guarding the black abyss underneath, of the orderly who pushed her down the hallway, was one of someone, something, not capable of such emotion. It knew only a few, and those were pain and suffering.

That didn't stop Sarah from screaming for help at the top of her lungs. The nurses and doctors ignored those screams as Raul rolled her by. They each stopped and looked at her as she rolled past. Some even leered at her. Cries exploded from the rooms they passed, "Sister, you have to get away," and "Sister. Don't let them."

Sarah agreed with both, but could not comply. For the fourth time since stepping on the island, she prayed. At first the orderly laughed at her. It was a hearty, full-body laugh that exposed more of the black abyss that was his mouth. She continued, and the crucifix around her neck began to glow. This caused Raul to lean back away from the gurney as he pushed her. He no longer hovered. She continued, and the light grew. An impact from a large force stopped both.

She remained conscious, thanks to the explosion of pain that shot through her jaw. A sharp yank cut her along her neck. Raul let out a painful yell and threw something on the gurney by her left hand. It radiated a familiar heat, and she smelled the start of smoke mixed with the burnt flesh. She opened her eyes to see Raul over her again, pushing her, but at times letting go of the gurney to rub his right hand.

"Please, let me go. I can help you."

His left hand delivered the answer with the force of a brick bat and knocked her unconscious.

# 11

Sarah woke up in a room under large bright surgical lights. She was still strapped to the gurney and her wrists and ankles were killing her. Her jaw was, too, which was a new pain she hadn't felt before. She heard water running behind her and her mind jumped to the scene she had walked in on before. The doctor was washing up ahead of a surgery, and she was the patient.

"Stop!" she yelled. Then she thought about it and added, "I am not even sick."

A creature cackled from the direction of the water. "Those that are sick rarely know they are," said a voice she recognized as the doctor. The water stopped, and she heard a mild rustling of fabric and then metal items behind her. "You, Sister, and I use that term loosely because I know who you are." She then felt it, and everything became clear to her. The summation of all the evil in this place rolled into one surged through her. It weighed heavier and heavier on her with every slow footstep she heard. The doctor. He was the key to everything. He was the demonic creature that haunted this island. Trapping and torturing all the souls who died on this island, both in life and in the ever-after. That explained the overwhelming vibration she felt. The sheer volume of spirits here, all calling out for help. They needed her help, or help from anyone, to be released and free from this one.

The doctor leaned over and leered down at her, "You have the worst sickness of all. Your faith. Your blindly believe in the existence of a benevolent being that will help everyone in their hour of need. Well, I have been here for many years, and seen thousands upon thousands of examples that disprove that. Every patient begged and beseeched your God for help. Each died. Never was there an appearance of an angelic being to save them in their final days of extreme pain and suffering. If you really think about it, it is all a big joke. They spent their whole life believing, but the moment they need saving, nothing happens. No miracles and no DIVINE intervention." He said the word 'divine' with a heavy weight of sarcasm. "Sister, do you have an explanation for that?"

Sarah wasn't sure if this was an actual question or more of a rhetorical one, so she said nothing, but he seemed to be waiting. She was sure there was nothing she could say that would change his mind. She didn't want to. She wanted to dispatch him and release all the others. Then the answer came to her, "God answers all prayers in his own way."

The doctor cackled again and threw his head back. The reaction was one she wanted.

"Not all answers are the ones you think he will give or want."

This caused another ear-shattering cackle. He regained his breath and leered down at her again. His smile wider, more defiant. "They have brainwashed you already. I expected more from you."

He leaned over. A cold finger scraped against her neck as it traced a line down her chest, across her sternum, and continuing across her abdomen. A set of empty dark eyes followed its path. The further the finger moved, the more evil and satisfied his smile grew. Raul approached with a tray and leaned over Sarah. The tray was placed down on the gurney just beyond her left hand. Her fingers attempted to reach it. Their tips felt the cold stainless steel edge, but no further.

"You are in luck, mental illnesses are my specialty. That is what I came to this island for originally. Not everyone agreed with my treatments mind you. Genius is rarely appreciated." He paused to give a quick self-appreciating smile. "When I found all of these other patients I expanded my practice. What doctor would refuse to help them?" His fingers once again traced the line down her sternum, but his eyes appeared unsure and he shook his head as he removed nis hands from her body. Sarah couldn't see where they were, but then felt them on her left temple. "I think right here is where I can start to cut the disease out of you."

Sarah prayed. It was the Lord's Prayer. Each word said with a sniff and a tear.

"Oh, my dear. That won't help you. Like I said. No one here was ever helped with any divine intervention." The doctor looked up at Raul and laughed. "But do it if you must. We can wait." He stood up, arms crossed, and looked on, annoyed.

She continued, pausing for a moment every few words to sniff. Occasionally letting a sob interrupt her prayer before she picked back up.

The annoyance that was on the doctor's face changed into a satisfaction. One that he shared a few times with Raul. "It is admirable. Even in the end, she believes her faith will save her."

Yes, Sarah believed her faith would save her. Of that she had no doubt. It wasn't the divine intervention the doctor believed she was asking for. She didn't need it. She had her own, and it had started to glow inside her left hand.

When Sarah reached for the tray, she felt something else that was in reach. A simple chain, which she knew the feeling of well. She found herself running her fingers along the links when she felt unsure. When worried or scared, she often let her fingers trace it to the crucifix that hung on it. Whether it was something real, a remnant feeling from the other crucifix she was used to, or just a silly belief, it always gave her peace. When Raul ripped it from her neck, her faith and power had been surging through it. The power seared his evil presence, and he'd discarded it carelessly within her reach. Slowly, her fingers pulled the chain closer to her. Each word of the prayer she uttered gave her another second to pull it even closer. When she finally felt the loop the crucifix was affixed to, she pulled the whole thing inside her palm to hide the first hints of light.

The more she prayed, the more it surged, from the words, from her faith, from her ability. It wouldn't burn her as it did the others, she was pure, she was one with it. She continued, and while they were distracted and mocked her from above, she slid her hand where she could just feel the harsh leather corner of the leather strap that held her down. Keeping her palm faced down, her fingers pushed the object until it touched the strap. A whiff of smoke carried the smell of melted leather up, and her hand quickly followed. She caught Raul under the chin. The point of the crucifix dug into the soft tissue and set his face ablaze. The blue flames consumed what remained of his tissue and torched upwards. Raul stumbled backwards, away from the gurney, before he fell into a pile of dust and was carried away by a puff of blue smoke.

Before the doctor could react, Sarah had her right hand free and pressed the crucifix onto his cheek. His skin sizzled, and he pulled back, running into the wall. She rushed to free her ankles and hopped down to the floor. Sarah took two steps toward the doctor, and then he slinked out along the wall and out the door into the hall. She knew why she was there, and what she must do.

With the crucifix dangling from the chain in her outstretched right hand, she followed him into the hall. When she stepped in, the disfigured nurses, doctors, and tortured patients were knelt down lining each wall of the hall, and the doctor ran down the clear middle. Each step more of a stumble than a sprint, as he looked back at Sarah often. She followed and watched him duck into the stairwell at the far end of the hallway. Before she reached it, the dank smell of death that had consumed her since she stepped on the island lifted and a light blazed inward through the windows of each of the rooms. Behind her, each of the patients, nurses, and doctors faded away.

Sarah stepped into the hallway on the second floor and didn't see any sign of the doctor. Instead, she saw nurses and patients knelt along the walls, like they were on the first floor, with one difference. Their heads were still bowed, but each had their right arm extended upward. A single finger on each of their right hands pointed to the ceiling. She turned around and looked at the next flight of stairs and knew where she would find him.

On the third floor, she heard leather-soled shoes slapping the tiled floor as he fled. She followed. Just as she saw on the first and second floor, the nurses, doctors, and patients had knelt on the floor. Where on the other floors, they bowed their heads silently, here they reached out for the doctor. A few grabbed at his ankles, causing him to stumble. Others lunged at him, but the old doctor jumped over them spryly. Only when one caught his ankle in midair did his body smack down on the floor with a thunderous boom.

They leapt on him like a hungry pack of wild dogs. Hands grabbed, ripped, and clawed at him while the whole mass growled. Despite their efforts, their weakened and decimated condition allowed him to stand-up and pull free. The mound of decaying humanity blocked his path and sent him limping back in Sarah's direction. She watched as he tried to pick up as much speed as he could when he approached her. She stopped, braced herself, and waited for him, like she had Jacob about ten years earlier when he rounded the corner into the dining room and she waited there with a sofa pillow in front of her to give him a good football style pop. There was no pillow here. This would hurt, and she knew it, but she was ready. The crucifix was firmly in her right hand.

The contact was harsh and violent. Sending both of them to the floor, and the breath out of Sarah's body. His shoulder caught her clean in the chest and sent her backwards, with him tumbling over her. To Sarah, it all appeared to happen in slow motion. She watched him flip up over her, and her mind commanded her right hand to reach up and touch any part of him she could with the crucifix. She caught him in the middle of his left thigh. His hands reached for the wound before his body landed on the floor and slid to a stop. A scream exploded from his mouth and echoed in the building, causing the panes of glass in each of the windows to explode outward in a shower of clear sharp death.

He struggled back up to his feet and, with a more pronounced limp, fled his pursuer. Sarah knew she had him and stalked after him. He went into the adjoining building that was the bell tower, and pulled himself up the ladder, hopping rung by rung with amazing speed.

Sarah stood at the bottom of the ladder, and realized she now faced the one thing in this world, both living and dead, that she was truly afraid of, heights. It wasn't the going up that bothered her. It was the looking out and seeing where she was and the down part that made her palms sweat and breath quicken. This created a hesitation at the bottom and on each rung as she climbed the ladder one at a time, each time telling herself, "You can do this. Its just a ladder." Inside, her mind responded by telling her it was a tall ladder that led to something really high up, with windows and openings she could fall out of. Not to mention the big opening the bell hung over.

# 12

At the top of the ladder, it was far worse than even Sarah's mind had pictured. It was a small square room. There were floor-to-ceiling archways in each wall to allow the sound of the bell out. The floor was nothing more than a four foot wide walkway around the opening, the bell hung just below them. A great wheel with a chain that dangled down was at their eye level. Sarah could only assume the chain ran all the way to the ground floor, to allow the bell to be rung from there. There was no way in hell she was going to look down the opening to check. She wasn't that curious.

The doctor was plastered against the wall opposite her and inched backwards away from her. He kept one eye on her, and the other on the edge to ensure he didn't take a misstep. A limp and grimace accompanied each step. The black-rimmed glasses he wore were in shambles. The frame was cracked, and they were missing one lens. His face wasn't much better. Black sludge oozed from deep gouges and scratches left by the mob. Fear ran through his eyes. He watched and jumped slightly when Sarah stepped off the ladder.

This was no place to get in a fight. Sarah had heard the analogy once about being in a knife fight in a phone booth. Compared to where she was now, the phone booth sounded much better. She had the advantage, if there was one. She blocked the only way out. As important as that was, she had to remember an equally important fact. If she stepped back into said exit, she would tumble down thirty feet to the third floor and her death. Not a good option.

She slid over, away from the opening, and plastered her back up against a wall, if she could call it a wall. It was a slim corner of brick. Sarah felt the hairs on her arm blow in the cool breeze that entered through the archway the left side of her body lapped over. Under her breath, Sarah said a prayer, and the cross glowed. The doctor saw that and shuffled back against the opposite wall, to increase the distance between them. The prayer Sarah said was not meant for him. She meant it to calm her nerves.

He looked nervously at the crucifix in her hand. Sarah surveyed the situation. This was a no-win situation. There was no easy way to approach him that he couldn't just slide around away from her. The mind is a wondrous thing. In the middle of a frightening and stressful situation like this, you would think the thoughts would be more focused. Instead, as Sarah thought of all the combinations of what could happen, her mind brought up the image from a cartoon of a cat chasing a mouse around and around this bell, never getting close enough to catch it. The image brought an awkward and wry smile to her face. She could see that happening.

To test her theory, she slid her foot along the walkway and, as if the doctor was her mirror image, his foot slid in the opposite direction, ready to move if she did. She didn't. There was no point. She wouldn't catch him, unless she rushed him. He was injured. No condition to run away from her. She could easily catch him, if the fear of falling hadn't paralyzed her. Then it hit her. She had heard of her father doing something once. Could she do the same?

She started praying again, and the crucifix responded. Inside, she hoped it would work the same as the family's cross. It wasn't the same object, and she didn't always need it, but she had never tried this before. She kept going until the entire room was illuminated, with a huge shadow of wheel and chain cast against the opposite wall. The doctor held up his arms against the glare. She felt she had done enough, but she didn't know. This was something she hadn't tried before. There was no way to know for sure except to try. It meant to take two leaps of faith. First, let go of the wall and her fear and bend down to the floor, and second, hope this worked.

Sarah took the first leap and, with knees quivering underneath her, she knelt down on the floor as close to the wall as she could. Her head had a clear view of both the hole in the center of the floor and the large archway. She tried not to look at either, but it was hard not to see the expansive view through the arch. If the fog were gone, Sarah assumed she could see both islands easily from here. Instead, she saw the collapsed roof of the chapel fifty feet below her.

She ignored the sight and pressed the crucifix on the wood floor, and continued to pray. Her voice wavered with her nerves. But the light was steady and crawled through the cracks of the floor. Slow at first, and then grew faster around the next corner and then the next. The doctor watched as it approached him and looked for a way out, but as Sarah continued to pray, now steadier than before, the light spread out behind her and approached him from the other side, too, trapping him where he stood.

He was trapped on an island of wooden planks with an incoming tide of something he feared most, the goodness and light of the Lord. The evil inside him hissed at the light like a great release of steam, and then the light made contact. His body shook violently back and forth and was mostly a blur. He was frozen in place. Feet locked to the ground where he stood. If there was ever a chance, it was now. She would need to move fast. Still unsure how any of this worked, she didn't know if he would be able to move as soon as she stood to move. She hoped it would last long enough.

Sarah stood up, lifting the cross off the floor. The river of light continued across the floor for a second and then receded away from her. She stepped cautiously back into the river, but just as soon as her foot touched the floor, the tide passed her. Sarah would have to move quicker, quicker than she was comfortable with. Her head felt woozy during the next few steps thanks to the large gaping arched window next to her. The next few had the security of the wall. She was losing her race with the light and needed to move faster still.

She rounded the corner just a step behind the illuminated path of salvation. The edge of it reached the doctor. His body continued to shake and twitch as he attempted to turn toward Sarah. His eyes widened as he saw her reach toward him with her right hand. It wasn't her hand he was focused on; it was what was in it. The crucifix. Sarah pushed at his forehead as he faced her. She saw his eyes, open wide, go cross-eyed as they remained trained on it and she pushed it into his flesh. It sizzled and he let out a scream for the ages that shook the room and caused loose particles of crumbling mortar to fall from the walls, producing a cloud of dust. Intermingled with the dust was the blue smoke that came from the spot of intersection.

"I condemn you from this realm for all eternity," Sarah declared. She pulled the crucifix off of the doctor and then pushed it in harder than before. "In the name of the Father," she twisted it until a blue flame emerged from the tissue. Underneath, the doctor flailed and writhed, unable to flee. "The Son," she pulled it back and then pressed it into a fresh area that sizzled and burnt in a blaze of blue smoke and flame. "And the Holy Ghost."

"I... I know what you are," the doctor stuttered.

"So do I. I am His vessel, to do his work in this place, and you are sent out of here."

With that, the light of the crucifix grew to a blinding level. Sarah held her left hand up to guard her eyes. The room filled with blue smoke, creating a blue haze that equaled the turquoise blue water that surrounded the island. A blaze of blue flame broke out all over the doctor, and Sarah pulled her hand back in fear of being burnt. She was still not sure if that was possible or not.

The doctor staggered a few steps forward, and then a few steps backward, before he lost his balance and fell inward toward the bell. Both feet lost their grip on the edge of the walkway and his body teetered over the edge. His head struck the bell, producing a deafening gong that sent Sarah searching for the closest wall to lean against. Both hands covered her ears, though that didn't help much. On impact, the doctor disappeared into a puff of blue smoke, and then he was gone.

Sarah inched away from the wall to look down to make sure he was gone. She saw nothing from her spot halfway to the edge. She needed to be sure and forced herself to take another step forward. As she leaned over, she heard a voice that sent her falling backwards against the wall. Her heart pounded in her chest.

"Sarah, be careful. No need for you to fall too," Father Lucian said. Behind him were the two sisters, precariously kneeling on the walkway and continuing to pray.

"Father! You almost scared me over the edge. Where did you go?"

"We have been here the whole time. Right behind you as you walked around the island. I assume based on what we heard you say, you found the doctor?"

"Yes, you didn't see it?" Sarah felt more confused at this moment than any time she had in the last several hours on Poveglia.

"Let's get out of here," Father Lucian said, as she looked out an arched window. "I am not fond of heights."

# 13

Sarah found coming down harder than going up. She had the constant fear of missing a rung with a foot and falling to the ground. Looking down as she stepped would have helped, but that wasn't an option either. The one time she tried created a slight spin in her head. She moved at a snail's pace, rung by rung. Each time searching inches at a time with her foot until she hit the metal bar. Then the other foot repeated that until it joined its mate.

Once firmly back on the ground, she, Father Lucian, and her two escorts walked down the hallway of the hospital. Its appearance was rather stunning to Sarah. For the first time she saw what years of exposure to the weather and wildlife had done to the interior sections. The only things alive here were the birds that had found a cozy corner here and there for a nest.

"Father, you didn't see anything?"

"No, Sarah. I could hear what you were saying, and I sensed it. It was strong, but I couldn't see anything. What did you see?"

"The hospital was alive with patients, nurses, and doctors. Most were trying to help. One brought in someone I think he'd dug up from the other island, to cut the disease out of him. After that, everything changed," Sarah explained. "It became dark and evil. The same patients were mutilated and tortured."

"Well, that makes sense."

Sarah looked at the father with an inquisitive gaze. "Why does it make sense? What happened to me?"

"Well, I didn't expect the island to pull you in like that, but it is not surprising. With your enhanced paranormal ability, you would have been an easy target for all of this to pull you in and show you its secret. What you saw was true. Those patients were tortured and mutilated, and the fact that you finally confronted him in the bell tower does, too."

Sarah thought to herself, *"I am glad it makes sense to someone."* Together, they all stepped out of the complex and back outside, where the boat captain stood inside the boat at the dock waiting for them, just where he had dropped them off earlier. Sarah now realized he had never left either.

"As I told you, this island was used as an asylum for those sick with the plague and then later, those that suffered with mental illnesses. Nurses and doctors did everything they could, but against such a disease, their efforts were useless. Nothing they could do would save a patient. That, as you can imagine, took a toll on their mental health. Most slipped into depression. Others slipped further. Dr. Damyan Nikolovich was the head medical officer of this facility in the 20s and 30s when it was repurposed to treat those with mental illness. Like the plague, it is not a disease that is often cured, which I am told took a great toll on him as well. He looked to extreme surgeries and treatments that in no way were approved by the medical community but, as you can imagine," Father Lucian raised a hand to the desolate facility before he continued, "over here, not many knew or were around, to object. It went unnoticed for years. He began to tell others that he was haunted and stalked at night by the spirits of those that he and the doctors that preceded him and jumped from the bell tower in 1930."

Everything made sense to Sarah. What she saw, what she felt. Why he was the focus of the evil she felt, and why the others tried to attack him once they had the chance. One thing still didn't fit.

"Father, what about the other island? I saw bodies smoldering over there. The doctor transported a man from there back to the hospital for surgery." She thought for a second and then came up with an explanation on her own that she floated. "Was there another building there that maybe burned down?"

"Oh, no. It is far worse than that. The island is where the ashes of every patient who died over here were scattered, following their cremation. It is the final resting place for over a hundred thousand souls."

# 14

"It was several weeks before I forgave Father Lucian for taking me there. It was a huge risk, and I was sure Abaddon was in control of me at times. Even after everything, I felt he had something to do with what I was able to do, but Father Lucian assured me that I was in control the whole time. That he and the sisters hadn't left the entire time. To me it was an extreme risk, and an unnecessary one. I was still trying to adjust to my life."

Ralph asked, "Why did he do it?"

"It was a test. To see if I could handle things. If I could handle my own fears."

"Looking back on it, do you feel you did?"

"I guess I did okay . We continued working together for many years after that."

"Did you," Ralph paused for a moment. His face contorted and his pen tapped his pad. Then he continued, "not sure what you call it, but I will ask it this way. Did you cure Poveglia?"

"Cure," Sarah laughed at the thought. "We don't cure. That is what doctors do. I always call it, putting it at ease. We released the presence that was there. That place will stay in ghost stories for years, but after we visited, there have been no more reports of anyone being injured when they strayed onto the island, and no stories of residents in the surrounding area hearing the bell sound."

"But the island is still closed off from the public?"

"Yes, that is a matter of the Italian government. What I understand is, they closed it off out of respect to those that lost their lives to the disease. Even placed a plaque there and cancelled a lease that was signed with a developer."

"One last question, if that is all right, Miss Meyer?"

"Of course," Sarah said. She could sit there and talk to these two gentlemen all day, but Mother Eliza gave them only one hour for this interview. Then Sarah must rest before returning to her duties there. One of which is counseling persons, and their family members, who had undergone some kind of encounter with the paranormal. It could be those that are afraid of a family member who kept coming back to visit, to some of her regulars that visit and speak with her monthly or even weekly. They are, like her, ones that had been, at some point, possessed by a demon. They are always appreciative of the unique perspective she can provide, but she always made sure they knew she learned a lot from them as well. Just because of who she was, and what she went through, they viewed her as the expert, but Sarah knew she was never through learning.

"Did you learn or take anything away from your visit to Poveglia?"

This was a very astute and insightful question. One that should require a great deal of thought but, for Sarah, the answer was obvious. She knew it the minute she'd realized why she was there, and what she was there to do. It went far beyond just what she was there for in that moment. It was much bigger than that. She knew her purpose in life.

"I took away my purpose. I am His vessel, to do his bidding in this realm," Sarah stated as a fact as clear as the sun coming up each morning. "That was when I knew I needed to devote myself and take the oath."

# The Stories of Sister Sarah

*Whispers of the Dead*

David Clark

# 1

"Good morning Ralph, Kenneth," Sister Sarah greeted the two young filmmakers who had arrived to hear yet another story from her life. Today they met Sarah in the convent's library, Kenneth's idea. After their first visit, Mother Francine gave them a quick tour of the grounds as they were leaving. The old tall wooden bookcases spoke to Kenneth the minute he saw them. The request was immediate, as was the acceptance.

They had planned to get there early and be setup when Sarah Meyer arrived, that was not the case. She was already there, waiting on them with her two ever-present escorts.

"Morning, Sister. I hope you slept well," Ralph returned the greeting and looked around the room.

Sarah saw this and knew exactly what he was looking for. "My brother will be along shortly. He is an early riser, but remember, this is early by a few hours, even for him." She walked around the room while her escorts stayed equidistant on opposite sides of the room. Her movements were graceful and smooth, not showing any effects of her many years. She turned and looked back at the library and said, "Kenneth, why don't you setup here. I can sit on that side of the table, and Ralph on the other, opposite me. The books will be a great backdrop, don't you think?"

Kenneth looked at where she stood and then back at the library, but only nodded in agreement.

"Come take a look?", she requested, and motioned for him to join her on that spot.

His wide-eyed reaction and gulp drew a smirk from Sarah. "Oh, come now. I am just an old woman. I can't hurt you, and you don't need to worry about him. Come on," she prodded.

After a few reluctant steps, Kenneth joined her on the spot. With a motherly touch, she gripped and turned his shoulders so he would see what she saw. Her hand pointed out the table and how the bookcase would frame the image of both of them talking quite well. He must have agreed since he retrieved the tripod and set it right there before starting to run the wires for sound, another old-fashioned touch. Like Ralph and his written notes, they also liked the sound and reliability of the older equipment. Similar to her father and Louis Tillingsly listening to old records from their youth, while she and Jacob rolled their eyes and pushed Bluetooth earphones in their ears to block out the noise. Her father swore the records sounded better than any digital copy. A point that Sarah didn't argue with at the time, but in later years she heard a few records and had to agree there was a richness and fullness that the digital copies couldn't produce.

The library was quiet, as libraries often are and should be. The occasional sound of a cord dragging across the cobblestone floor echoed through the chamber. Kenneth's tripod let out a squeak while he twisted the collar to tighten the neck to lock it in place. He paused at how loud it sounded and the four sets of eyes that focused on him. Resuming slower this time.

"Sorry I am late," Jacob said as he entered the door with a creak.

"Not a problem, lazy boy," Sarah said with a smirk that reminded everyone that deep inside all of us are the children that still will poke fun at a sibling.

When he entered, Kenneth was almost finished setting up and Ralph and Sarah had taken their spots. Sarah spotted her brother looking around the library for where he might sit. She patted the seat next to her. "It's all right, I hope?" she asked Ralph.

"Of course, Sister. Whatever makes you most comfortable."

Sarah smiled and reached over with her left hand and slid the chair out for Jacob. With no hesitation, he walked to the chair, took off his overcoat, placed it over the back of the chair, and had a seat.

"Shall we?", she asked.

Ralph looked at Kenneth, who said, "Ready." A red light turned on at the front of the camera aimed at the three at the table. The lens turned ever so slowly to bring them into focus. "All yours, Ralph."

"Sister Sarah, thank you for seeing us again."

"My pleasure," she said.

"During our last discussion, you told us about your visit to the island of Povelgia. That was your first time out with Father Lucian on, what the Vatican called in their book, a mission to restore faith."

Sarah giggled at the term, an uncontrollable response that she caught before it continued for any prolonged period. Some might consider it disrespectful. A part of her did, but it was something she couldn't help. The Church had gone far enough to acknowledge the existing of ghosts and the keepers, but still danced around admitting to, or using the term that best described what they really did, exorcisms.

"What I would like to discuss today is something that occurred seven years later."

"You want to talk about St. Augustine," she interrupted.

"Yes, how did you guess?", asked Ralph with a dazed look on his face.

"I have been on over one hundred missions," she managed to say without a laugh, "most were rather non-descript, so I am sure you are not here to talk about those. There are several that are more interesting. St Augustine was one of them."

"Yes, it was very interesting. It was the first time you worked with your Father, but more interesting, the first recorded interaction between the Vatican and law enforcement."

"And solved three murders," Sarah proudly added.

"Yes, wait. Three?", Ralph asked. Surprise was written all over his face. Kenneth looked up from behind the camera. Jacob sat back in his chair and crossed his arms.

"You didn't know about that, did you? Not all the details were in what the Vatican wrote. There are a few that neither myself, nor Father Lucian, told them. It wasn't necessary. See, even back then, I knew the day would come when the secrets would be let out, and some secrets need to be protected."

Ralph motioned to Kenneth, who turned stopped recording. "Sister, are you ready to tell those secrets now?"

Jacob leaned forward, bracing his forearms on the table as he turned to look at his sister. A palpable tension flooded the room. One that Sarah cut, not with a knife, but with her signature amused laugh that she had had since she was a little girl.

"In a way. I can tell you the story without exposing anything that should be protected. If that is all right?" She looked at Ralph for agreement, but the look was a grandmotherly one that conveyed she wasn't really asking for an agreement, she was telling.

"Of course." Ralph waved Kenneth back behind the camera and when the red light came on he continued, "Sister, tell us about St. Augustine."

# 2

Sister Sarah stood over a sink with her sleeves rolled up to her elbows and soap suds halfway up her forearms. In front of her, enough baking trays to bake bread for an entire army sat soaking. It was not an army the Sisters of San Francesco were feeding; it was the town. Twice a week, every week, they spent the morning baking bread before heading into town to deliver it to the elderly, sick, and needy.

When Sarah had first arrived, she'd confined herself to the baking side of this task, and of course the cleaning, which made the scene before her a common one. It took four years before she finally trusted herself enough to venture into town.

During their visits, the Sisters delivered nourishment for both the body and the soul. Her first visit to town was also the first time Sarah had delivered a prayer to someone other than herself. It was something she'd expected to feel odd, and it did, at first. The way the kind eyes of the older women had looked at her from below her curly locks of silver hair had made Sarah hesitate. The woman expected the touch and word from the divine, and Sarah felt anything but either. She felt tainted and unworthy to deliver such words and comfort. Then Sarah remembered how those words made her feel and started. The words flowed out of her with meaning and feeling, just like they did when she said them for herself. It felt natural. Sarah took the oath two years before, but she hadn't performed any public duties before that moment. Doing that one task made her feel whole.

Sarah's waterlogged hands resembled those of an older woman, hands like Mother Demiana, she thought. There was no disrespect, just something she noticed as she looked at her own after handing the last of the baking pans to Sister Francine. It was nearly noon, and they both, along with Sarah's ever present escort, had been in the convent's kitchen since just after six in the morning. Behind them, Sister's Maria and Nanette were bundling the bread in towels and baskets for the afternoon's delivery. A simple knock on the door signaled a visitor that was not just one of the other sisters. They wouldn't have knocked, and instead would have entered to take care of whatever task had brought them to the kitchen.

Each stopped what they were doing and directed their attention to the door. Father Lucian entered, holding his wide-brimmed black hat against his chest.

"Father, it is great to see you," beamed Sarah. She dried her hands and proceeded over to give him a hug.

The rest of the sisters stayed where they were and greeted him with a "Good day, Father."

"Its good to see you, Sarah. Baking, I see."

"Yes, Father. It is Thursday," she said. "What brings this visit?"

"Let's talk somewhere else. I need your help, if you are up to it."

There was a murmur in the background, and Sarah looked around to see her sisters smiling and giggling. Sarah's exploits over the last six years had made her a celebrity, not something she wanted, yet not something that had gotten out of control. To date, Sarah had assisted Father Lucian in twenty-seven cases, solving twenty seven paranormal mysteries and disturbances. Some had even called her a real-life version of the Father Dowling, but she paid it no attention. The outings were what she viewed as her penance for what she'd caused and what she was. Not to mention, she quite enjoyed them. There was a thrill of discovery in each one. The discovery of something within herself and, of course, the truth. "Of course, Father. Lead the way." She hung up her dish towel and followed him out, her escorts in tow. Inside, she knew the trip she had so looked forward to was now not in her future.

"What is it Father?", she asked as they walked side by side down the narrow hallway and out to the central courtyard. He sat on the simple wooden bench. Sarah wanted to join him, but instead picked the bench across the circular bird bath from him, to ensure there was room for the others. She didn't have any idea how long they would be there and had always considered them in such matters.

The midday sun was high in the sky and didn't cast many shadows. Those it did were short. It felt warm and rejuvenating on her face. Father Lucian's face wasn't in the sun like hers was. The setting, and the deep distress she felt inside of him, accentuated the lines and creases of his features. She wasn't telepathic or empathic. She could only feel those not living, but in her years of service she had developed an educated sense that told her when someone was troubled. Her gaze studied him through the tumbling water that bubbled up in the fountain on top of the birdbath. Two swallows were taking full advantage of the refreshing drink.

"There has been an incident," he said, and then stopped.

"Father, there is always an incident," she started and then she caught herself. Could something have happened to someone she knew? That was always a fear, and being so far away, she may not receive word directly. Father Lucian would be the obvious choice to deliver such news.

"Father, is everyone all right?", she asked, a touch of a tremble in her voice, her hand raced to her heart.

"Yes, they are all fine. In fact, they may be helping with this," he said with a distant stare before righting himself and adjusting his posture to sit up straight and look right at her. "We have a job to do, but this one is different, I am afraid. There has been a murder and, well, to my own surprise, the authorities are pointing to something from the unnatural world and asked for help. Of course, you know who that falls to." He held his arms out wide and then pointed to himself and across to her. "Now, I have seen a great many things tied to death. Possessions, and even exorcisms that have gone wrong, but this is something new for both of us. This victim, based on everything that they have presented me, was not possessed, or even aware of the paranormal world. They were targeted and murdered in, if you can believe it, cold blood. No motivation, that anyone can find."

"Father, this would have to be a demon. A normal spirit couldn't," she stopped and then corrected herself, "wouldn't do anything like this. They are tied to events and other spirits. Unless..."

"There is a connection," Father Lucian interrupted. A smile crossed his face, which Sarah had to assume was a show of his approval for how far she had come. "That is what they want us to find out. To determine if it really was a spirit or demon that did it and find the connection. Remember, even if it is a demon, there has to be a purpose. They don't just kill for the fun of it. Everything has a purpose."

"That is true. So when are we going?"

"Well. We need to leave now. The jet is waiting for us as we speak."

"Oh," she sprang up. "Then I must get my things. Where are we going?" Sarah started for the hallway that led back to her room.

"St. Augustine, in Florida."

Sarah stopped in her tracks and turned. "St. Augustine?"

"Yes, know it?"

"I do. I went there," she started, and then thought better of the explanation. Being a Sister of the cloth made it seem inappropriate to talk about that spring break trip her and Charlotte had taken to Daytona when they were twenty. "I visited there once."

"Well, you are about to visit again, because that is where we are going." Father Lucian pushed up from his bench. "My things are already in the SUV, and the driver is waiting. Speaking of waiting, your father and Father Murray will be there when we arrive. They are both on their way now to do some pre-work on the area, and to calm the local authorities."

"And Jacob?", she asked, with hope in her heart.

"I am afraid not, dear. He is staying home to tend to the farm and things there in Miller's Crossing."

As disappointed as she felt at hearing Jacob wouldn't be there, her insides were all a flutter at the thought of seeing her father and Father Murray again, and she practically skipped back to her room.

# 3

"Dad," Sarah screamed as she ran through the doors of the Fly-By Cafe of the Northeast Florida Regional Airport. Her father stood up from the booth just in time to catch her in his arms. Her momentum shoved him backward against the table, jostling the glasses of water and two cups of coffee he and Father Murray had enjoyed as they waited for Sarah and Father Lucian to arrive. The elderly priest slipped past the two of them and stood waiting, next in line for a long-awaited embrace. Edward had visited his daughter several times, but Father Murray hadn't seen her since she left Miller's Crossing. When Sarah let go of her father, she jumped over to Father Murray. Edward continued his greeting with a hardy handshake and pat on Father Lucian's shoulder. Her two escorts remained at the door. The sight of a priest and three nuns entering the small airport cafe in this rural portion of northern Florida town drew the looks of those sitting in the booths enjoying their tuna melt or a slice of what the sign said was fresh baked apple pie. Sarah had to believe this was a first for this place.

Father Murray and Edward led them outside to the waiting van. It was white, with double doors on one side to provide access to the two bench-style seats in the back. Black lettering on the side said, Cathedral Basilica of St. Augustine Youth Ministry. Sarah looked at it, and then at her father and Father Murray, then back at the van, and another look, with a smirk, at the two men she had known for years. "I leave you guys alone for a few years, and you start stealing vans from churches."

Father Murray sniped back, "Hey, we are left without your good influence, Sister. Actually, we are just borrowing it while you are here. We needed something large enough to transport everyone."

Edward held open the back door for her, like he had when she was a child. "I wish Jacob could have been here," Sarah said as she stepped in and slid across the bench.

"He wanted to, but the harvest is coming and he had a lot to do. He is obsessed," Edward said.

"It's better than being possessed," Sarah said with a laugh. She meant it as a joke, but the stares she got from everyone, including her escorts that had slipped into the bench behind her, told her she'd failed. She felt as uncomfortable as she had that time she let some gas slip out in a quiet class room in the fifth grade. Every kid in the room had looked at her before exploding with laughter. There was no laughter this time. "I am joking, ha ha," she said, and she could swear she saw a few of them let out a long exhale before getting in the van themselves.

They drove down US 1, also called the Dixie Highway, toward the downtown area. Sarah had stopped here on the way back from Daytona and noticed how touristy the whole thing looked for a small town. Coming back these many years later, she found it hadn't really changed much. You had old homes and buildings from the Spanish colonial area, mixed in among modern gas stations and mini markets. Some of the buildings were still homes, but had been converted into bed and breakfasts. Each advertising how old they were on a brightly painted wooden sign hanging off a post or porch banister. The stores were much the same. Old homes fashioned into small clothing stores, with people in period clothing standing outside to invite you in. A contrast to the occasional modern looking office.

The closer you were to the waterfront, the more lost in time you became. Entire blocks were closed off from traffic, preserving an area much like it had been for almost four hundred years. As the traffic crept past those roads it left Sarah to wonder. A story her father found in an old diary said the first Meyers were smuggled in by the Vatican, through St. Augustine. Had they walked those roads, maybe stayed in one of the inns that still stood there. Or were they housed in the cathedral that stood behind it, by the central plaza? This was a piece of her history she appreciated.

"Detective Borrows wants to talk to us first, before we go to the museum," Father Murray told them. "He will meet as in Constitution Plaza, the site of the old historic market."

"What have you been able to find out?", asked Father Lucian.

"Well, you are in one of the oldest cities in the country. So as you would expect, there are ghost stories on every corner," said Edward.

"And ghost?", Father Lucian asked.

"Yes, there are," Sarah said. They were there, she knew it, she felt it. None close at the moment, but they were in the area.

"Oh, yes, and a sprawling ghost tour business. We even went on one last night."

"You what?", Sarah asked, exploding forward in her seat to push her head up between Father Murray and her father. "Say again?"

"Well, what your father said isn't completely true," Father Murray confessed. "We went on two."

Sarah exploded back in her seat. Laughter rolled out of her in a way it hadn't in longer than she could remember. Father Lucian appeared to share in the humorous nature of what they had both heard, and chuckled himself.

"It was research, and we had the time," her father tried to explain.

"Let me get this right. Two of the most legendary ghost hunters in the world took a ghost tour?", Sarah asked, barely able to form the words through her laughter. She watched from behind the two men and saw even Father Murray's shoulders rise and drop a few times as he laughed.

"It would seem so, but we had a point to it."

Sarah gathered herself and attempted to contain her laughter while she listened to Father Murray's explanation.

"What we were asked to look into was no unimportant matter. We wanted to find out what kind of local legends may exist that could drive the fear and speculation that a poltergeist did this. You know better than anyone, Sarah, how much some of those legends can shape opinions."

He was right, she knew. Her family was the center of most of those legends. "Okay, then, what did you find?"

"Well, there are a ton of different legends here, such as, if you look out the window at the fort, Castillo de San Marcos," Father Murray said with his best attempt at a Spanish accent. "They say at night it is not uncommon to see Spanish soldiers patrolling the wall, or a Seminole Indian jumping off the top of the south-west wall. And then, over there, see that second-floor balcony? They say you can hear the clinking of mugs as the ghosts of bootleggers that used to frequent it, around the turn of the century, sit and enjoy a drink. Everywhere you look there is a story, but none larger than the other. No central, what I would call bigfoot or ghost of St. Augustine type story, which is what I was interested in learning. It seems everyone here believes, or is open-minded, but unlike our little place, they can't really see or know for sure."

"And the museum?", Father Lucian asked.

The two men in the front shared a look between them before Edward said, "I think it would be best if you walked through it first, before you are told the story. We heard the story first, and are concerned that may have clouded our judgement."

They continued along the waterfront and turned away from the water, instead of following the traffic over the ornate Bridge of Lions, to a rectangular tree-filled plaza with several monuments, a gazebo, and a large, covered structure which was the old market.

Edward pulled into a rare empty spot and the four of them got out. Sarah paused again, enjoying the sensation of the fresh breeze coming in across the Matanzas River. They were close to the ocean, she knew that. She could see the slight change in how the sky looks over a large body of water, a reflection of the light off the water and, most of all, the smell. That familiar salt smell riding on the breeze, that you only smell around the ocean. The last time she had smelled it was on a small island in Italy.

It was sunny and warm, but not overly so. People were out walking along the sidewalks that traversed through the park. Families with small kids who would stray back and forth from the concrete to the grass. People on their lunch break, hurrying along. Couples walking hand in hand, without a care for time. Sarah found her gaze following them. Not in a longing sense. At one time in her life, she'd wanted to be one of them, but she knew now that was no longer an option. Just a dream from a life that seemed so long ago. A relationship between the three of them would never work out.

Sarah and her escorts rejoined the others in the present and followed them into the park. Father Murray and Edward led the way, and greeted a man wearing a navy blue suit, paisley tie, and a lanyard around his neck with a badge swinging from it. He was a tall, thin man, but not gangly. He had a good three inches on her father, and would have a good six or seven on her. As she approached, she heard her father handle the introductions. "Detective, this is Father Lucian, and my daughter, Sarah," Edward caught himself and then corrected it with a nod toward her, "Sister Sarah."

Sarah, never forgetting her protectors, looked behind her and introduced Sister Mary Theresa and Sister Cecilia. "They are with me," she said.

"The Vatican representatives?", he asked. His voice was as syrupy smooth as a used car salesman, with just a hint of a southern drawl that might be best heard sitting on a porch telling stories while drinking one too many. Sarah's escorts had his attention. They stood six feet behind her, praying the whole time.

"We are," Father Lucian answered sternly.

"Are they okay?", the detective asked. Pointing at the two sisters behind Sarah with a hand that held a burning cigarette.

"They are fine," Father Lucian answered.

"Okay," he said, wearily at first, then moved his focus to Father Lucian. "Father Pedro wasn't sure y'all would take us serious enough to actually send anyone." His eyes caught the two sisters again, and his head turned to look right at them over Sarah's shoulder. "Are you sure they're okay? Why are they praying? That is praying, right?" he asked with his nose crinkled up, producing several lines on the bridge between his eyes.

"Yes, detective," responded Father Lucian. "It is their order. Go on."

"I want to make myself clear. We aren't the kind of department that believes in, or searches for, things that go bump in the night, but you live around these parts long enough you hear and see things. Sometimes you have a case where nothing from the natural world makes sense. That is when those things you hear and see creep in, and the otherworldly fills in the blanks." He looked around for a minute. His foot playing with a rock in the dirt, rolling it back and forth, back and forth, creating an indentation it would fit in easily. "Heck, probably anywhere else if I tell someone I need to talk to a priest about my case, or even hint at what I was going to suggest, they would take my badge and gun and laugh their asses off as they escorted me out."

"Understood, Detective. What can you tell us?"

# 4

"Well Father, two weeks ago, this past Thursday, a body of a woman was found burnt in the restricted upstairs quarters of the museum. She was forty-seven-year-old Lauren Middleton, a local. She was part of the tour through the museum. Most saw her and remembered her at the beginning, and various times throughout the tour." Detective Burrows reached inside his jacket and pulled out a picture and showed the others. "As you can see, she was striking, so the sort of person people remember."

The detective was right. Lauren had striking blue eyes that seemed to jump right off the picture at Sarah while she studied it. Curly black hair framed her pleasant rosy face. Her features appeared to be the sort that couldn't frown if she tried.

"What was the source of the fire?", Father Lucian asked. Both Father Murray and Edward looked on with heavy anticipation, and Sarah wondered why.

"There was no fire. Not even the slightest hint of smoke."

Sarah now knew why her father and Father Murray had the looks they had plastered on their faces.

Father Lucian's head flinched backwards. "I don't understand," Father Lucian explained.

Sarah had been through many odd situations with Father Lucian through the years. Demons, poltergeist, lost souls, those messing with things they shouldn't, such as black magic, and a few Sarah didn't know how to characterize. Even the two-year-old that sat with him once and calmly discussed the hierarchy of demons and where they fit in it, all the while quoting "Pseudomonarchia Daemonum" the whole time. Nothing ever appeared to surprise him. In fact, he appeared to rather enjoy the debate with the two-year-old. This had him off kilter.

"Father, there was no fire. Nothing burnt, but her. Mind you, some of the exhibits in that place are old and non-replaceable. They tune the smoke detectors to go off if a person strikes a match. Nothing went off. They found her, two days after the tour. The cleaning crew found her while doing their weekly pass through the upper floor, which is off-limits to guests."

"Could she had been killed and burnt somewhere else, and then brought back?", Sarah asked, looking for a logical explanation. Their presence there hinted to her that these had been worked through, but she needed to ask and be sure. One thing Father Lucian had always reminded her during her training, don't be so quick to the conclusion that the paranormal was involved with a situation. Sometimes, many times, there was a logical explanation. It was a hard lesson for her to learn to apply, but eventually became second, well maybe third, nature.

"We considered that. That was until we watched the security footage. Cameras cover every door, window, and the entire parking lot. There is no way anyone could leave or enter that place without being on camera. She never left, and definitely wasn't snuck back in like this." Detective Burrows pulled out a second picture and passed it around. "Before you ask the next question that I imagine is in your mind, yes, those are burns."

Sarah winced and her stomach turned at the gory sight. Only her stark blue eyes remained unburnt. Everything else was charred black.

"What about the smell?", Father Lucian asked.

This question sent Sarah's stomach into another somersault. She knew exactly what Father Lucian was asking. Burnt flesh has a rather distinctive and putrid odor. It was one Sarah had become familiar with on her first mission with Father Lucian to Poveglia. Since then she had encountered it twice. Fire, and incineration, are important symbols in their world. It was seen both as a cleanser and destroyer. Set a person on fire, and you cleanse the soul. It had been used for hundreds of years, through every period of religious persecution, all the way up through the Salem witch trials. The other side believes fire to be the great destroyer, the rapture's lake of fire. Through all of her case studies, Sarah had noticed demons often used fire as a way to manipulate the living. Each had something in common with what she saw. The fire damage often disappeared, and when it didn't, only the target of their action, the person, was scarred, as if it was a blemish on their soul.

"No smell, either. Not in the building. Once we removed her from the building, the smell of burnt flesh was overwhelming in the coroner's office. By the way, his report said she was burnt from the inside out."

Sarah spied her father looking at them, smiling, as her brain worked over the details to the ultimate conclusion. There was no natural explanation.

"Suspects?", asked Father Lucian

"Well, no," Detective Burrows fumbled. He looked down at the rock he had worked over before and restarted the task. "I mean, we checked a list of her family, friends, coworkers, and exes a few dozen times." His head shot up and his eyes narrowed. They were in the shade, so that wasn't to shield from the glare as he looked around at all four of his visitors. "Look, we checked out all the normal stuff, and there was nothing. No suspects. No motive. Hell, how do you even burn someone from the inside? Is that even physically possible? We are kind of going out on a limb to bring you guys in on this, but there are no answers in our world for this, and things just line up."

"Line up with what?", Sarah asked. Her curiosity was more than piqued.

"Hold up, detective," Father Murray interrupted. "I think it would be best for them to walk around the museum and get a feel for things before they hear those details. They need to have a clear point of view."

# 5

After dropping off Sister Cecilia at the church, where quarters were made for each of them, they proceeded to the museum. Sister Mary Theresa would be her daytime escort, and Sister Cecilia would be responsible for Sarah at night. Having only one at the convent was a common occurrence, and only recently had she started to venture outside those protective walls with only one. Not that there wasn't someone there to help if something happened. Either Mother Demiana or Father Lucian were with her on each of those excursions, and they could more than manage her.

When they arrived at the museum, Sarah and Sister Mary Theresa marveled at the outside of it. To say the building was eclectic would be an understatement. On the outside, it appeared to be a miniature version of the old Spanish fort just down the road. Inside, it was a combination of old Spanish home and turn of the twentieth century styling. Right down to the rich usage of the colors red and yellow in the furnishings in the non-public entrance, spaces used only by the staff, and for the ghost tours. The museum itself had been closed since the incident happened, and yellow crime scene tape was still wrapped around the handles of the large doors where the general public entered.

The office entrance had remained mostly closed as well. Only opening for the local police investigating the murder, and then Father Murray and Edward the night before. Wendy Marcus was the person who opened the doors each of those times, she now opened them for a third time. Her official title was curator, but as Father Murray explained on the ride over from the plaza, it was more general manager. The museum of oddities had added nothing new in years, and the decision to do so, as well as the decision to rotate any exhibits to and from another site, could only be made by the corporate entity. Not to say she was not well versed in the history and story of the building and every exhibit. She had to be, as she served as a tour guide as well.

"Shall we start the tour?", Wendy asked. Her hands were clasped in front of her, and Sarah noticed the cherub face on the squat woman took on a serious but well-rehearsed look. She was about to start her show.

"Actually, Mrs. Marcus," Edward started, but was interrupted.

"It's Miss, and just Wendy."

"Okay, all right, Wendy. I think it would be best if they just walk around on their own first and get a sense of the place. If that is all right with you?"

"Well," she said with a bit of a huff. "I guess so." She moved aside, out of the doorway, deflated.

Father Lucian took off his wide brimmed black hat and handed it Father Murray, "Father?"

"Of course."

Then he, Sarah, and Sister Mary Theresa passed by Wendy and into the hallway that led straight into the museum. This was not like any museum Sarah had ever seen. It was case upon case of the strangest objects in the world. Skulls of deformed creatures. Beaded fertility necklaces. Paintings done on the head of a pin, which Sarah stopped and squinted through the magnified glass on the display case to see the image. The detail was unbelievable. So unbelievable she thought it might be a hoax, with the picture painted on the glass instead, but when she looked she found clear glass.

Each room opened back into a central opening that ran to the ceiling. A forty foot tall motorized Ferris-wheel, made from erector set parts, stood proudly in that space. Its cars rotated up and around slowly. One after another, over and over again. They continued, together the whole time, past a full-sized picture of a man who had body modifications performed to make him look like a lizard, and through the room dedicated to pirates, obviously themed because of the history of St. Augustine itself.

"So, I wonder what piece in this place is haunted?", Sarah asked as she studied a wall lined with burial masks.

"I doubt it is that simple," replied Father Lucian.

"Yep," agreed Sarah. She knew it wasn't, she felt it, and could tell he did, too. She walked around and studied the exhibits like a tourist, though she would argue it was part of her investigation to try to learn what they were dealing with. Father Lucian avoided the exhibits and instead kept his path to the center of each room. There was something there. That was an undeniable fact. Sarah had felt many things since she stepped off the plane. St. Augustine had ghosts to go with all of its ghost stories. That was a fact. The museum had its own story and ghost, or possibly ghosts, to go along with it.

On the third floor the feelings became stronger and wasn't just a "something", and had now manifested itself in the all too familiar pin-pricks on the back of her neck. They grew stronger the further she moved in the third floor, past an optical illusion of a woman in a shower. From one angle she was there, from the other she was gone. Sarah stopped, prompting Father Lucian to ask, "What is it?"

Sarah held up a single finger at first, and then stood dead still, listening, feeling. It was there, with them. Not on that floor with them, but close. It was above them, in the space blocked off to the general public. The floor where the victim was found.

Sarah sprinted around, the heels of her shoes thudding on the wooden floor. Each thud echoed. She was searching for something, some place. The place where the feeling was the strongest. It would be there that she could reach out and sense the most, possibly even see it, if it wanted to be seen. If it didn't, she had her way to make it.

At first, the far northeast corner seemed to give Sarah the strongest feeling, but as she moved around, she found the center of the room was equally as strong, but different. Walking back toward the first corner, Sarah felt that feeling fade, but it never went away completely. It changed, or merged, and became something, or someone, different. There were two entities. She was sure of it. One above them in the center of the room. The other above where she was now. That was the only explanation for the two spots and the two slightly different feelings she felt.

"There are two," she reported to Father Lucian, who paced from the far corner along the wall to the door and back.

"I agree. One right here, by the door, and the one you have over there."

"No," she said, confused by what he said. If there was one by the door, that would make three. She didn't come through that door that lead in from the hall, but instead entered from the neighboring room. Sarah joined him by the door, and just as he reported, there was something here. It was unmistakable, and it was strong. The tingling she felt up her neck was just on the verge of being painful, like a dozen needles jabbing in and out of her skin. There was something else, too. A darkness that appeared to drip down from the ceiling toward her. "There are three."

"What?" Father Lucian stopped his pacing and spun around toward Sarah.

"Yes, Father. One in that corner over there," she pointed to the opposite corner. "One in the center of the room, right under the light, and this one here. The others aren't as strong or dark as this one. This one is evil."

Father Lucian made long strides across the room. Each step echoed in the room. When he reached the center he paused, but only for a second. Then he continued on to the other corner, where he paused again and then spun around on his heels before marching back to Sarah in the doorway.

"I see. I can feel them, but can't feel anything specific."

"I can't either, just the malevolent intention of the one here. I am still too far away to sense any more, or to see them."

"Then we need to fix that," Father Lucian said and then headed off.

Sarah and Sister Mary Theresa followed him in and out of every room on the floor, headed for what she had to assume were the stairs to the floor above them. The building was a maze of normal rooms and others that had been reconfigured to funnel you in a certain direction and out the other end. They found themselves turned around many times, retracing their steps, before finally reaching the back stairwell they had used to come up from the floor below. The problem that now faced them was the locked door that blocked them from going any further. Father Lucian shook on the knob of the door, and Sarah noticed something. This door was not part of the original structure. Everything else in this building was old. Solid wood trim, plaster, and solid wood doors. This door was metal and rattled as he pulled on it. The surrounding walls flexed a little against the strain. They were drywall, not plaster like everything else. They had sealed this stairwell off, but why?

# *6*

"Miss Marcus," Father Lucian called as he hurried down the hallway back toward the office.

"It's just Wendy, Father," she reminded him.

"Wendy, can you open the door to the stairs up to the top floor?"

"Oh, no can do. We are under strict orders to only open that for cleaning," she said with a hint of authority, as if to remind everyone there that she was the curator.

"Who can?", he asked. "It is imperative that we get upstairs."

"It's not part of the tour."

"This is not a tour, it's an investigation," he said.

Sarah could tell, based on her experience with Father Lucian, he was growing frustrated. His hands became more animated as he spoke, instead of staying rather docile, and the pace of his words. While he had always tried to stay level-headed, or at least give the appearance that he had, she could always tell he was frustrated when his speech sped up.

"Wendy, remember we are here at the request of Detective Burrows," Father Murray added.

"Well," she said. He voice waffled in tone to one more subdued, defeated. "I guess you are. You mustn't touch anything up there. All right?"

"Yes, agreed. We won't touch anything."

She stood there for a second, lost in thought, before she turned back toward the office. "Let me get the key."

"Sarah, what did you find?", asked Edward.

"There are three spirits up there. Father Lucian and I both felt them."

Father Murray laughed and reached into his pocket, pulling out his wallet. He reached inside with a smirk on his face, searched for a moment, and then pulled out a five-dollar bill, handing it to Edward.

"Thank you very much, Father," Edward said. He shoved the bill into the front pocket of his pants. "He thought he only felt two, but I insisted there were three," explained Edward. "One was evil."

Sarah high-fived her father, "You still have it."

Both Father Lucian and Sister Mary Theresa appeared to be rather amused by this. It added a jovial sense to the moment, but that ended just as quickly as it appeared when Wendy re-emerged holding a single key up from a ring with what had to be every key to every door known to man on it. She held the one specific key they needed between her forefinger and thumb, allowing the rest to dangle below them.

Wendy walked right past Father Lucian's outstretched hand. It was obvious she had no intention of handing the keys over to anyone else, and marched through the hallway back toward the stairs. She led the parade up each flight, one step at a time, with the keys held out in front of her as if it were a lantern lighting the way. The dangling keys jingled with each step. The sound in the cavernous stairway resembled the rattling of a chain. A sound perfectly at home in a haunted house.

The parade reached the metal door leading up to the top floor. With the key still firmly between her forefinger and thumb, and the pinkie extended on that hand for no reason Sarah could figure out, Wendy turned to face them, and reminded them with a scold, "Now, remember, touch nothing."

Father Lucian nodded, but that didn't appear to be good enough as she looked around him to the others, waiting for an agreement or nod from all, even Sister Mary Theresa.

The key slipped into the lock without resistance, and Wendy turned it. In the silence of the surroundings, the clink of the metal pin and barrel in the lock was easily audible, especially when they all slid into position, opening the lock. Wendy turned the handle and pushed the door inward. A gust of stale, foul burnt air rushed out and past Sarah, rustling her hair and her habit. Which she found odd. Nothing moved on anyone else. The curly red hair on Wendy, who stood directly in front of the door, didn't even twitch.

Wendy pulled the key out and let the door open the rest of the way inside and then reached to the wall and flicked on the lights. In front of them was an ash wooden staircase, like the others in the building. The inner wall was plaster, which matched the rest of the building.

Father Lucian stepped forward to enter, but Sarah reached forward and grabbed his elbow. He stopped and looked back at her. "Let me go. I want a chance to go up there alone."

There was no objection, which Sarah hoped was a sign of the trust he had in her. She moved forward and entered the stairs with Sister Mary Theresa behind her.

The stairs creaked as they stepped up each runner, all the way to the top, where it opened up to a long hall with rooms lining either side. It all resembled an apartment or hotel. Shadows of numbers still appeared on the doors. Sarah walked carefully down the hall, making sure she was aware of what she felt, no matter how faint. The layout of the floors below them had turned her around, messing up any reference she might've had for which room they were below when they'd sensed the spirits. She stopped in front of two doors on either side of the hall from each other. Room sixteen and room seventeen. Cold pins pressed slightly into her skin from each side, and Sarah felt two distinct entities pulling at her. They were in those rooms. Of course they can't be in the same room, she thought to herself. Which room now was the decision that she pondered.

For no particular reason, her hand reached and turned the door handle for room seventeen. It opened. Again air rushed out with the smell of burnt wood. Sarah stepped inside and let her hand search the wall beside the door for a light switch. It found one that felt foreign to her touch. It was round, not flat against the wall, with the switch in the middle. When the light came on, she saw a room that time had forgotten. Everything from the bed, with the large wooden headboard with shelves built into it, that Sarah had only seen on old re-runs of *The Brady Bunch*, to the lamps on the night stands with the large hoop shades. The heavy usages of browns, light greens, and mustard yellow in everything screamed late fifties. As she walked across the room, Sister Mary Theresa entered behind her. Sarah didn't see the spirit in the room, but it still pulled her inward further, and toward another door. She turned the handle, opening up the bathroom and there, sitting on the edge of the tub with the shower curtain pushed off to one side, was the flickering image of a woman, blonde hair pinned up shoulder length, wearing just a towel wrapped around her body. Her legs dangled in the tub full of water.

"Close the door," she asked. "Close the door or he will come."

At first Sarah didn't know who she meant, and then she remembered the dark presence she'd felt below. That could be who the woman was referencing, but if it was, she had news for her. A door would not stop him.

"Please, close the door," she wailed. Her hand trembled while holding the towel closed around her chest.

Sarah rushed back to the door that led out to the hallway and closed it to appease the woman. She then needed to spiritually close the door to protect. She still didn't know exactly what they were dealing with. Sarah motioned for Sister Mary Theresa to come closer to the bathroom door and then pulled a vial out of her pocket and sprinkled the holy water in an arc behind them and continued in through the bathroom door, around the tub and back out. This practice that she had learned a few years ago from another Keeper worked best if you did it in a circle, to help focus your abilities, and to protect you from dark elements. Since then, she had used it a few times, and not always in a perfect circle, so she had faith this would work.

"He can't hurt you now," Sarah said to the woman.

In between flickers, the woman looked fully alive to her. She had full lips, high cheekbones, and glowing skin. A woman that would be called a true beauty, and she was young. Probably not much older than Sarah herself. Her big brown eyes looked at Sarah and at Sister Mary Theresa standing in the doorway. She appeared calmer now.

"Thank you. I should have never come here." She then mumbled something that Sarah couldn't fully make out, but one word was clear, "Warden".

"What was I thinking?", she said. A hint of tears glistened down her cheeks. A hand delicately reached up to wipe the tears away. "I am not that kind of woman, mind you. Not one of those hussies that frequents hotels for this kind of thing. This was just a one-time thing. An impulse, really. A simple and stupid impulse."

Sarah approached the woman, flipped down the top on the toilet, and had a seat. The woman watched her, like she was welcoming a friend, no apprehension or fear. Instead, she sat on the edge of the tub, now using the corner of her towel to dab away the tears.

Being closer now allowed Sarah to see her in greater detail. There was a depth to her. The curve of her jawbone. The high point of her cheeks. The line her collarbone made just above the towel. Even the texture of her skin showed signs of someone who was chilled, maybe after getting out of a warm bath into the chill of the room.

Sarah felt the chill, too. A combination of the spectral image in front of her, and the draft she felt in the room. The woman continued to sob and looked at Sarah and then away, out the window behind the tub. The waning moments of daylight were melting into the night, leaving a red hue. Sarah reached over and took a tissue out of the box. A puff of dust rose up in the air and followed her hand as she handed it to the woman. Before Sarah knew what she was doing, the woman took the tissue from her and said, "Thank you."

"You have nothing to fear. The door is closed. He can't harm you now," Sarah said.

"I know. It's not that. I am just stupid. I should have never come here."

"Why is that?", Sarah asked.

"I barely know him," she said, as if talking out loud to both herself and Sarah, not wanting to answer the question.

"Who is he?"

"I met him over coffee, just today. He mentioned he had a room here and asked me to come back with him. I was so foolish," she said, staring out into space the whole time.

"It's okay. Really. We all do foolish things."

"I guess we do. We are just human, aren't we, Sister?"

"Yes, we are. Why don't you tell me your name?"

The woman started to speak, and then stopped. She sniffed the air and stood up from the tub. Fear dripped from her eyes as she ran out of the room screaming, "No!" Just then, Sarah could smell what the woman must have. It was putrid and burned her nose, like gasoline or some kind of lighter fluid. Then the hint of smoke wafted in along the ceiling, like a cloud that grew. Sarah ran out of the bathroom and into the inferno that was the outer room. She looked back at Sister Mary Theresa and was about to yell for her to run, but then noticed she was calm and showed no signs of being aware of the fire around them, or the immense heat that radiated from it.

The woman ran back into the bathroom and the door slammed behind her. Sarah attempted to open the door, but the handle wouldn't turn. Behind it, the woman screamed. The terror in her voice chilled Sarah's blood. The walls vibrated around Sarah, and the bathroom door exploded open, blowing her to the floor. She ran and found the woman lifeless below the water in the tub. A black smudge covered her throat. Sarah reached down and pulled her head up above the water. A weak gasp escaped her mouth, and she said in a wispy voice, "I didn't know he was married. I didn't know." She said it over and over while the water in the tub disappeared. Her body turned into a blackened figure and then a pile of ashes that were carried away by the smoke.

Sarah walked out into the hall and, on faith, stepped through the flames. They were all around her, but did not burn her. It also consumed the hallways and adjacent rooms. The heat was getting to Sarah, and she stood there considering seeking out the other spirit for more answers, or heading back down the stairs. A wall of flames behind her sent her moving forward to the stairs. When her foot hit the top stair, the flames were gone, but the scent of freshly burned wood and flesh remained.

# 7

Halfway down the stairs Sarah stated, "There was a fire up there."

Wendy Marcus answered from just outside the door, at the bottom of the stairs, "Oh, no, dear. That is what is so odd about that woman. There was no fire up there," then she stopped and looked at the others. A finger came up and met her lips as she appeared deep in thought. She went to speak, but stopped before a sound escaped her mouth. By the time Wendy spoke again, Sarah and Sister Mary Theresa had made it down the stairs, but remained just inside the doorway. "Well, there was, but that was over sixty years ago, in 1944."

"Really?" Sarah stopped two steps from the bottom. "Did it have anything to do with a woman and some guy she came here to meet, named Warden?"

Wendy let out a nervous giggle and then motioned for Sarah to come out. When Sarah didn't move, Wendy's hand movements became more exaggerated as she stared at her. She slammed the door shut and quickly relocked it as soon as Sarah and Sister Mary Theresa exited. Her waddle away from the door was hurried and agitated. She didn't wait for the others, she reached the stairs and headed back down. Sarah thought she was mumbling as she did so and ran after her.

"Miss Marcus, I mean Wendy, what is it?"

The rotund woman didn't stop and bounded down the stairs with her curls and body bouncing with each step. She descended with purpose. Sarah didn't need any special training to tell she was running from something, something disturbing and frightening. It was obvious, her mind was on one track and that track led as far away from what was up those stairs as she could get, as fast as she could go.

"Wendy?", Sarah called again, but the woman didn't even acknowledge her.

Sarah then rushed down the stairs and squeezed past her, jostling the woman slightly against the rail. On instinct, Sarah apologized as she passed. On the next landing she stopped and waited for the woman, blocking her way. Sarah looked into her eyes as she often did when counseling someone who was dealing with trauma. It was a tip that Mother Demiana had given her, that seemed to instantly open someone up. A psychological trick, she'd said. There was something about the eyes of a nun looking at you in full habit that made everything all better. Sarah had yet to see it not work, this was no exception.

"Wendy, tell me what has you so frightened, my child." Sarah asked, even though Wendy had a good fifteen years, if not twenty, on her.

"It can't be," Wendy stammered. "Please tell me you know what this place is."

"It's a museum," Sarah answered, her gaze looking into the woman's bright green eyes. They shivered with fear.

"No, dear. The man's name was not Warden. You are in the Warden. This was a hotel before it was a museum, it was called the Castle Warden Inn."

Castle Warden Inn. The name and what the woman said made sense. She didn't come back with a man name Warden. She came back to the Warden with a man. That was when Sarah knew why the woman came back, and why she seemed to regret it and feel foolish. She may have even felt embarrassed talking to a nun about following a strange man back to a hotel for a sexual rendezvous. That made sense, but what happened next didn't, so Sarah asked, "Was there a fire in the hotel?"

"Oh dear, oh dear," the woman stammered and worked her way past Sarah, onto the landing. She didn't go down the next flight of stairs. Instead, Wendy searched out the closest chair she could find and had a seat. Her head buried itself in her hands. "So, you guys really can talk to ghosts?", she asked, her voice muffled and weary.

Sarah knelt down in front of Wendy and placed her hands on Wendy's knees, and with a calm and soothing voice she said, "Yes. Father Lucian, Father Murray, my father, and I can see and speak to ghosts. We can do more, too. We help people that are troubled by spirits, and help those spirits find peace. They have asked us to look into what happened." Sarah felt it was important to leave out the battles with demonic entities they often found themselves involved in, to keep everything feeling as peaceful as possible. "Now, what can you tell us?"

Wendy's head emerged from her hands. Her face was flushed, and she took a few deep breaths as she sat up. "Now, I don't believe in such stuff, but in a place like this you hear and feel things. We have all smelled smoke at various times and just learned to ignore it as one of the oddities in the history of this *odditorium*. Some of the other workers have said they have heard the voices of one of the women wailing about following him back here, and how stupid she'd been." Wendy stopped and just shook her head, "I always just chalked it up to the stories of this place playing with their mind. Yes, there was a fire here. That is a fact, and the story behind this place. This building was originally the Warden Castle Inn. It was built in the 1880s by William G Warden as a mansion for his large family. They lived in it until 1926, and it sat vacant until 1941, when it was sold to Marjorie Rawlings and her husband, you know, the woman who wrote the book "The Yearling" from over in Crosscreek. They turned and made it a really nice hotel, adding some of the amenities the Warden missed. She started inviting people she met down, and it took off. Then, in 1944, it all came crashing down. There was a fire in the upper floor that killed two women. One a Bette Nevi Richeson, of St. Augustine, the other was Ruth Pickering, from Savannah." Wendy stopped again and looked at Sarah with a light behind her eyes.

"You know, we have a pamphlet downstairs with their pictures on it, if you would like to see them."

"I would," Sarah said.

Wendy led them down to the office while she recounted the rest of the story. "Now, there are two versions of the story, and no one knows the truth. One version has it that a mysterious Mr. X killed both women and set the fire to cover it up. The problem is, other than the fire, the police found no other cause of death. Not to say the 1940s police, in a small town like this, had a lot of experience in investigating mysterious deaths."

She walked down the hall, back to the office, telling the story the whole way. Even as her voice faded into the distance, and behind walls in the small office, to retrieve the various stacks of pamphlets that would normally be stacked out in holders on a business day, for guests to take and read through as they toured the property. She started flipping through the stacks. "The other version is a little more salacious. See, Mrs. Rawlings was a little bit of a unique person, and folks say you never knew which person you were going to get. She spent a lot of time up north and elsewhere, away from her then husband, Norton Baskin. He ran the hotel and was known for his all-night poker games, and other exploits, to keep him entertained while she was away. Some say he had rooms on the upper floor reserved for women he would invite up. As you can imagine, she might not approve if she arrived home and found some 'special guests' staying. Wait.... here," she said and shoved a red folded pamphlet at Sarah. On the cover were two old black and white pictures. One was the woman Sarah had spent a few minutes talking to before the floor erupted ablaze. The second was the spitting image of their victim. "The truth behind the mystery was never solved, and it was chalked up to an electrical fire in the hotel. After that, it sat empty for a while before Ripley's bought it."

It wasn't the picture of the woman she had talked to that drew Sarah's attention to the pamphlet. It was the second picture just below it that caused her to quickly pass it around to the others, pointing to it as she handed it to them. The woman, a raven-haired beauty with striking blue eyes, had an uncomfortable resemblance to one Lauren Middleton. The two could be twins, separated by a century.

# 8

"Could it be that simple?", Father Murray asked from the back of the group.

"It could, very easily. I have seen it a few times," said Father Lucian.

"The Moors in Somerset?", asked Sarah.

Father Lucian merely nodded in agreement.

Wendy looked at the group as though she was a tourist in another country, watching the locals talk, without understanding the language. Her gaze watched everything, but her ears were just waiting to hear her name.

"Three years back, I think, Father Lucian and I assisted another Keeper on a case in Exmoor National Park, in Somerset. There was a spirit that was attacking hikers that were out exploring the moor. If you have ever thought about exploring a moor, don't. They look like beautiful prairies and meadows from a long way off, but they're full of thatch, holes of mud, and everything else that makes hiking in one unpleasant."

"Sarah," Father Lucian prompted.

"Oh, sorry," said Sarah with a quick roll of her eyes. "Anyways. There had been more than three dozen mysterious attacks in this National Park, all in the same general area. The location was not the only coincidence. They were all female. All hiking alone, and all mid-twenties, blonde, medium build, with brown eyes. Not a brunette in the bunch. It took a while to research local legend and deaths in the area, and we found one. A man, Donald Ward, from the late nineteenth century, who died in the moor. See, he went hunting in the moor with his dogs after he found out his wife was having an affair with another man in town. The dogs returned, but he never did. They searched the moor for two days and never found him. Some speculated he didn't go hunting at all. They believe he went out there to commit suicide, out where the moor would absorb his body. Whatever the cause of death, suicide, or something more natural, I have no doubt that place would consume the body in a way it would never be found. You can probably guess what his wife looked like. She was a mid-twenties blonde, with brown eyes."

"The trouble with Mr. Ward," Father Lucian interrupted, as he moved to the front of the group. "He never showed himself to anyone that didn't resemble her. So, as you can imagine, no matter how many times John went out there, he never saw him. Neither would we, if Sarah hadn't found a way to flush him out."

Edward looked at his daughter with one of grave concern and worry. The kind of worry that weighed your soul down. "You didn't let it..."

Before Edward was able to complete the sentence Sarah shook her head no and then directed her father's attention to her attending escort, Sister Mary Theresa. Who knew all eyes in the room had moved to her, but she kept praying the whole time through the slight smirk on her face, under her blonde hair and brown eyes. Sarah had to use her as bait to call him out. Once he was out, she was able to feel his presence and make contact. He wasn't a demon, just someone with a great deal of pain that was taking it out on who he thought was his wife. This was probably something similar, but who was the attacker? And why?

"I don't get it," Wendy said.

The entire group turned to look at the puzzled expression on her face. She stood there, slack-jawed, and looked back and forth at each of them. Sarah was the only one who stepped forward, bringing with her the pamphlet. Standing beside her, Sarah handed Wendy the pamphlet and pulled her attention to the second picture. Sarah waited for the light to go on, and when it didn't, she applied a little pressure to the switch with a question, "Recognize the picture?"

"Of course. The first picture is Bette Robertson, and the second is Ruth Pickering, the two women killed in the fire. I don't understand." Wendy looked up at Sarah, like a student asking their teacher for help.

"Do you have a computer?"

"Well... yes. Back in my office."

Sarah followed Wendy back, looking through the doors of each office. The one at the end of the small hall still had a light on, and that was the one that Wendy went into to retrieve the pamphlets. It was a rather small office. Just big enough for the desk in it and the single guest chair that sat in front of the desk. If you were a guest, you wouldn't be able to slide it back farther, and you would need to scoot between it and the desk to sit. Marks scarred the wall behind it, where some hadn't realized that and slammed the chair backwards into it. On the far corner of the desk sat a docked laptop. Sarah sat down in the chair and attempted to roll the chair closer, but it didn't move. It couldn't, there were no wheels. She reached down and grabbed the seat and jerked it forward, causing the legs to chatter against the floor. Wendy stood on the other side of the desk, watching.

"You don't mind, do you?", Sarah asked.

Wendy said nothing to stop Sarah as she pulled up the web browser and went to the local news site. In a few clicks she found the story which had Lauren's picture under the headline. Sarah turned the laptop toward Wendy and held the pamphlet up next to it.

"Oh, my god," gasped Wendy. She stumbled back into the guest chair, sending it into the wall behind her.

# 9

Sarah reemerged from the office, leaving Wendy standing in the office doorway looking back out at them like she had seen a ghost, or had been told of a one. Sarah had told her what she planned to, needed to do. After seeing Ruth's picture, Sarah was convinced this was a case of mistaken identity, of the paranormal kind. It is well known that spirits can latch hold of places that are familiar to them, that is why they typically stay around, or what others call haunt, their homes or other buildings that hold a particular importance to them. The same holds true for people. No one knows for sure if emotions and memories remain once you die. Sarah hopes they do. She couldn't imagine not remembering her family after she is gone. Something about that sounds more like hell than heaven. There were cases after cases of a spirit interacting with someone that bore a similarity with someone they knew when they were alive. Sometimes the encounter was nothing more than lingering close to the person, causing them to get the "creeps" or feel the occasional chill, and others were of the more violent type. In those cases, whether they intended to do harm was not known. It could be as simple as just being the only way they knew how to reach the person from the other side. It didn't matter, Sarah dealt with them the same way.

When Sarah explained to Wendy what she needed to do, the woman sat there and stared at her in disbelief. A common expression when Sarah tried to explain such things to someone outside of their "special order". As Sarah kept explaining the "what and why", Wendy's arm rose. Not in a deliberate move, but more subconscious. The keys dangled from her hand. Sarah said, "Thank you," when she took them.

"What now?", Edward asked.

"I have no doubt the dark spirit we felt is the man behind the murders of the two women, and he attacked Lauren because she reminded him of Ruth. I need to remove him from the situation, permanently, or he will attack the next woman that walks through here that looks like her. It's not like a dog going nuts when it hears the doorbell, you can train them out of that behavior. With a spirit you have to remove them," explained Sarah as she led the parade back up two flights of stairs to the metal door. She turned the key and opened the door. The smell of freshly burnt wood and flesh wafted down the stairs and past her. She didn't need to wonder if any of the others could smell it, she already knew it was just her. Just like nobody else could see the last billows of smoke dancing around the light that hung over the stairs.

Leaving the others behind. Sarah and Sister Mary Theresa ascended the stairs for the second time. From behind them Father Lucian asked, "Did you sense the dark spirit when you were up there?"

"No," she said, stepping up another tread on the staircase.

"Do you need any help locating him?", he asked.

She paused on the next step to the top and turned around, "No, I have his room number." Sarah turned and stepped up on the landing and disappeared around the corner. Sister Mary Teresa followed her.

It was true, Sarah had his room number, or what she hoped was the room number. Wendy had told her that Mr. Baskin used room thirteen for his all-night poker games, and for his extracurricular activity. It would make sense that he would be there. As she walked down the hall, she passed room seventeen and felt Bette again, just like before. The room on the other side of the hall pulled at her, it was room sixteen. Sarah had every intention of continuing down to room thirteen to confront and deal with Mr. Baskin, but found she couldn't. Every time she attempted to step past room sixteen, something stopped her. It wasn't some spectacular paranormal force that trapped her feet to the floor. It wasn't a demonic presence putting up a spiritual barrier that she couldn't cross. No, it was something much simpler than that. It was her own curiosity. She wanted to go in and see, meet Ruth Pickering, so she did.

The door to room sixteen was not locked, and it opened easily. Like the room across the hall, it was trapped in time with the same mustard yellow and green decor. Sitting on the made bed, with it's mustard colored comforter, was a flickering Ruth Pickering. She was dressed in a periwinkle blue dress with matching buttons running up the center, matching shoes and hat, and white gloves. Two small brown suitcases sat next to her feet on the floor, all packed. Her striking blue eyes looked at Sarah as she walked through the door.

"Morning Sister, are you here to help me with my bags?", Ruth asked. She tugged at the hem of her dress, pulling out any wrinkles.

Sarah pondered that question before giving an answer. She gave every appearance of being all packed up and ready to check out. Perhaps that is how she was when the fire broke out, and she was now stuck there for all of eternity. Sarah knew that was something she could help with, "In a way, yes, I am."

"Good. That man down the hall has been making a commotion with the woman across the way all morning. I have to admit, some of what I have heard makes the thought of walking out into the hallway alone uncomfortable."

"Do you know the man?", Sarah asked.

"Oh, no. I have never seen him in all my life. I can tell you, he seems to have a temper and a mouth on him. All the swearing and pounding on the door." Ruth pursed her lips together as if the thought of what she had heard was sour to taste.

"So, they have been fighting?"

"All morning, and I am not talking about what most people would consider morning. I mean, from the time the clock rolled over past midnight." A single finger wagged at Sarah as Ruth spoke. Sarah could tell she had had enough, but was also concerned for her own safety.

"Could you tell what about?", asked Sarah, wondering if one of the reasons Ruth may have felt concerned for her own safety was because she had heard something she shouldn't.

"This and that. Mostly sounds like a lover's quarrel, even though there was nothing that sounded loving about it. It would seem she had a change of heart and he didn't agree, if you know what I mean. Some topics should be discussed behind closed doors, if you ask me."

"I completely understand," Sarah said.

"Good. Let me grab this one, and you can grab the other and I can get out of here before they start the noontime show," Ruth said and then bent down to grab the smaller of the two brown leather suitcases.

"Tell you what," Sarah started. "Why don't you just stay sitting right there for a few minutes. I want to go down and talk with him to make sure we won't have any more trouble from him, and then I will be right back to get you. Is that okay?"

Ruth let go of the case with a little thud. She sat back on the bed, her shoulders were no longer the straight back and proper posture they had been, they had a bit of a slump to them. Her hands joined one another on her lap, they were in constant motion, ringing each other out. "I do have places to go," her voice dripped of the same level of disdain her body showed.

"I promise. It won't be long. I feel it is something I need to do for everyone's safety," explained Sarah. "Is that all right?"

Ruth looked away from Sarah as she considered it. She looked back, but not at Sarah, around Sarah. Everywhere but her eyes. "I guess so," she said, rather tersely.

# 10

Sarah left room sixteen and headed down the hall for her next destination, room thirteen, and the man the ghost stories referred to as Mr. X. She felt his presence as soon as she passed the door for room fifteen. The sensation overwhelmed any residual tingling she'd had from Bette or Ruth. It was a different feeling altogether. The tingling and pricks on the back of her neck were there, and the hairs on her arms were standing up, but that was all normal. There was a weight, a heavy weight she felt pushing down on her, and an overwhelming claustrophobic feeling that made her want to duck below a low ceiling, even though the ceiling was still four feet above her head.

The closer she walked, the heavier the weight, and the closer the walls and ceiling became. A heat radiated toward Sarah, and she prepared herself for another wave of fire to rush past her, engulfing the entire floor like before. Such displays would intimidate most, but Sarah had seen this many times before. After the first wave hits her and she realizes they, and any pain she felt, were not real, she just ignored them.

The heat and weight were oppressive when she reached the door. As she reached for the knob, she wondered if both were meant for her. Was whatever behind the door aware of her? It was possible, since both Ruth and Bette were. This could also just be a normal state for anyone that approached. She looked behind her at sister Mary Theresa, who was doing her duty, showing no signs of any discomfort or effect. Sarah knew the dedication of her sisters, and considered that she might not give off any outward indications, so she asked, "Stai bene?"

Sister Mary Theresa nodded.

"Senti calore?", Sarah asked again, to be sure.

This time Sister Mary Theresa looked up from her prayer, and paused for just a second to say, "Nessuna sorella."

"Okay," and Sarah turned the knob.

There was no great fire inside, just another room like the others. Same colors and interior decorating theme. Same furniture. A man's sports coat lay on the bed and a pair of black leather shoes sat on the floor beside the bed. The man that wore them was nowhere to be found. The sound of water running in the bathroom, and steam coming out past the partially closed door, hinted at where he was. A valve squeaked, and the water shut off. Sarah heard the sound of metal scraping on metal.

It sent shivers through her body. That sound, and the sound of fingernails on a chalkboard, had always been the two that made her skin crawl. If someone ever really wanted to torture her, all they would need to do is trap her in a room with that sound. This particular sound was one she recognized. It was why she'd swapped out the shower curtain rings in her bathroom with plastic ones.

The bathroom door opened and a middle-aged man with dark hair walked out. A towel was wrapped around him from the waist down. His hands worked another towel through his hair and over his face. To say he looked surprised after he lowered the towel and saw Sarah standing there was inaccurate. He appeared shocked, and stammered for a few moments, just looking at her as he took a step here, and another there. He appeared to gather himself and righted his posture. It even appeared to Sarah that he sucked in his stomach and puffed out his chest. Not that it did much. The man's physique was far from being considered out of shape. Broad shoulders, a nice well-defined chest that led to a tight and rippled abdomen that trapped a few remaining drops of water from his shower. He threw the towel over the arm of a nearby chair.

"Going to church on Sundays isn't enough? You guys are now offering a delivery service, is that it, Sister?", his tone cut through the room and cut through Sarah.

"No, sir. I am here to help," she said, trying to keep it simple. She still felt all the normal sensations, as well as the heat and weight, but couldn't tell if this was just a spirit or if there was a demonic presence here. There was no need to tip her hand and have the situation turn messy, yet.

"Help," he chuckled. "The help I need is something you can't provide." He walked over and retrieved a white undershirt and pair of boxers from an overnight case sitting on the maple wood bureau. His gaze locked on her.

"I hear there were some problems here this morning, and I want to smooth things out for all involved."

He chuckled again. But this had an acidic tone to it, and the weight of the air around Sarah increased, bearing down on every inch of her.

"You want to smooth things out? What exactly do you want to smooth out, Sister?" He leered at her and threw the undershirt in a ball of fabric onto the bed. She hadn't noticed how harsh his eyes looked before. She had to assume they were brown, but the color was so dark they looked pitch black, like pieces of coal swimming in a sea of white. "You are kind of cute, for a nun. Maybe you could smooth something out," he said and flashed a cigarette-stained smile at her and dropped the towel.

Without even a quiver of shock in her voice, Sarah responded, "Not in that way." She stepped forward, her hands together in front of her. "I feel you are someplace you shouldn't be, and your presence here is hurting people. I can help you find your way home." Sarah decided to go ahead and pitch it out there and see if he would take the easy way.

"I am right where I need to be. What is it, Sister? Have you never seen a naked man before? I know you guys take some kind of oath," he walked toward her, being sure to exaggerate the movements of his pelvis as if he was putting on a show for her. "Vow, that is what you call it," he corrected as he snapped his left hand.

Sarah asked, "Sir, why are you here?"

"I think you know. Of course, my stay would be better if she hadn't found her conscience and turned me down." He jerked to a stop and looked at the wall to his right before jerking his head around toward Sarah. "I think I finally figured out what your deal is, and why you are here. This is all your fault."

The air pushed down on her with a crushing force. Sarah's knees struggled to support her. The heat that was there now pulsed hotter and hotter.

"This is your fault. You talked to her and gave her some kind of moral dilemma. I don't give a shit about your morals," he exploded, and threw both hands into the air. Then he lunged for his overnight case and threw it against the wall. Both hands grasped his face. He glared at her through his fingers before one finger shot forward toward her, "What is it with you people? You and that nosy bitty down the hall. You think you are better than everyone and can sit in judgment. I know I heard her whisper, judging me. Each time she cracked open the door to see me and Bette talking in the hall. What, were you in the room with her, or the next room?" Distraught, he ran around the room, shoving chairs and tables over. His clothes were strewn all over the floor, pieces hung from the lamp, casting an eerie dark shadow on the wall behind him. It appeared to grow as the heat intensified. "I have worked too hard for what I have. I won't let you ruin this for me."

# 11

The man ran to his case that now sat at the base of the wall next to the nightstand. Its contents scattered along the floor. He picked up an aluminum bottle and ran toward Sarah. She jumped out of the way, slipped, and fell to the floor. His naked body ran past her, and through Sister Mary Theresa who stood in the doorway. The dark shadow that was on the wall followed behind him, along the floor and out.

Sarah rushed to her feet and followed. A very terse, "move" escaped her mouth as she approached her escort, who was unaware of what was happening around her. When she got to the hallway, she spotted him standing at the edge of the stairs, pouring the liquid on the carpet. He continued down the hall, past both rooms seventeen and sixteen. Sarah's nose burned and eyes watered. There was no mistaking the pungent odor of the fluid. He continued pouring the fluid and slammed Sarah against the wall as he passed by, continuing the line down the hall. It extended from the stairs halfway down the hall, just past his own room, which he ducked inside. Before Sarah reached the door, he was back out in the hallway with a chrome-plated lighter. He had already struck the flick to produce a flame. He stood there appreciating the glow which cast his facial features into an evil light.

"There is no reason to do this," Sarah said.

"That is where you are wrong," he sniped back. "There is every reason to do this. You, that busy body down the hall, and the tramp I brought with me, won't destroy me."

"You have already been destroyed. It is time to stop this and free yourself. Stop tormenting yourself and others," Sarah pleaded. The dark shadow left him for a moment and smacked into Sarah. She crashed into the wall. Its weight held her there and pushed harder until the plaster behind her cracked. She heard and felt the crack behind her. A shot of pain exploded from her ribs and caused her to wonder if one of the pops she'd heard was something inside her giving way. She screamed, and the force clamped down harder, pushing what air remained from her lungs. Each gasp for air only brought in fumes that burned her lungs.

"Stop. I won't let you tear apart everything I am," he declared and dropped the lighter onto the carpet. The line of fluid exploded in a blue wave that progressed from one end to another, before spreading out along the floor. He ran, still naked, into room seventeen. The shadow released its hold on her and followed the man. Sarah, feeling bruised from head to toe, rushed in after them. Through the bedroom and into the bathroom, where Sarah found the man with his hands around Bette's throat, forcing her under the water in the tub. She fought with all she had. Each time her head breached above the water, a scream escaped and filled the room.

Sarah went to intervene, but was too late. She reached to pull him away, but he turned toward her and grabbed her around the throat. Sarah kicked, pushing him away long enough to allow her to crawl to her feet. He caught her ankle before she reached the hall and slammed back to the floor. His touch produced a pain unlike any she had felt before. Another strategically placed kick to his forehead freed her again. His touch blackened her skin with soot.

Sarah pulled her way into the hall, but again, he was on her and pulled her back. He climbed on top of her, adding to the oppressive weight her body felt. Both hands grabbed her throat and wrenched back and forth, increasing pressure with each twist. Her breath was being ripped from her as her outsides were being burnt. Over and over, he repeated, "You won't take everything from me." The flames spread up the walls around her, to the ceiling above. To her right, she heard Ruth screaming as the fire ravaged her room.

"You are not a bad person. You just made a mistake. God will forgive you," Sarah croaked out in between gasps for breath. Smoke filled her lungs. She needed to cough. A task his hands wouldn't allow.

He retorted with a sinister smile, "I don't care about your God, Sister." The dark shadow grew over him. It could have been columns of black smoke, but she felt the evil grow.

"His glory will accept you into his kingdom for life ever after," she mumbled, in between two hacks to expel the smoke that invaded her airway.

He flickered and disappeared for a moment before reappearing. The crucifix around her neck began to glow. The light hit him in the face, and he leapt off of Sarah. Sarah pulled herself against the opposite wall. Every breath a struggle. She reached for the crucifix and basked in its warmth and comfort. On her knees, she crawled over halfway and faced him.

"He does not judge, for we are made in his image. Our flaws are his flaws. Whatever mistakes you made in this life won't cost you anything in the afterlife. Accept his truth and light in your heart, and you will join him." She used the crucifix to outline a cross in the air in front of him. A blast of heat and smoke shoved her back against the wall. Her head whipped backward, cracking the plaster. Behind him was the dark shadow again. It stretched up the wall and across the ceiling.

"This is not your vessel," she yelled. The shadow continued to creep toward her. Again, she directed her attention to the man, "Accept him into your heart and cast out any ill agents that whisper mis-truths and falsehoods into your ear. There is only one Lord, one Savior. Accept him and enjoy peace and love in the afterlife."

The man looked at her, eyes clear, full of fear. He appeared to attempt to mouth "How?" The shadow receded across the ceiling in a flash and entered him. The clarity she saw in his eyes was gone. The pits of darkness were back, and they gazed upon her with all the ill will in the world. Then he leapt at her. It wasn't a move, a leap, or a jump. A force launched his body at her.

Her mind said, "The hard way." She stood up and met it with a punch, sending it sprawling down the hall. It came at her again, and she dodged its attempt, landing in an ocean of flames that didn't burn her. The only one that had been burnt was the man. Sarah had contacted his chest with the crucifix as it flew over her. The spot sizzled and blue smoke wafted up from the wound.

It continued to sizzle as it made another pass. Again, Sarah hit him with her crucifix. This time, his body crumpled into a mass on the floor. She had done more damage, but was not unscathed herself. It got a good swipe in that time, down the center of her back. The pain had her lying flat on the ground.

Sarah struggled to push up off the floor, but collapsed after each of the first several attempts, from the pain. Through her tears, she watched him as he attempted to get to his feet. Finally she powered through the pain, making it to her knees. Then, one leg at a time, she made it to her feet and walked toward him. His body was twitching and contorted in unnatural ways. His chest was flat on the ground, but his face looked straight up at hers. He growled at her from deep inside his chest, while his mouth said, "I accept him."

"If only it were that easy now," she said as she knelt down next to him. "You accepted evil into your heart, and I must cleanse you."

Sarah placed the crucifix on his forehead. He writhed at its contact. The growl deep inside grew, vibrating the floor. "I cast you out, agent of evil, unclean spirit. Leave this vessel, for it is not yours." A blue flame exploded from the spot the crucifix touched and ran down the length of his body, filling the hallway with blue smoke. His body turned to ash and then faded away, as did the flames from the fire he'd started.

Sarah stood up from where she knelt. The pain in her back was gone, as were the soot smudges from where he had touched her. She had dismissed him, so he wouldn't bother anyone again, but she didn't feel her work was done yet, and went into room seventeen, into the bathroom. Bette laid there in the tub, motionless. Sarah knelt beside her and gave her her last rites. Her presence flickered once, slowly, and then faded away. There was one more task for Sarah to do.

Ruth Pickering sat on the bed right where Sarah had left her earlier. "Are you ready to go?"

"Well, I didn't pack up for the health of it."

Sarah sat next to her and took her hand. "You were trapped here through no fault of your own. You are one of our Lord and Savior's creatures and are now allowed to return to him. Do you accept him into your heart?"

"Yes. I do and always have."

# 12

"I will say, looking back at all that now, it was rather intense. It wasn't my only time dealing with multiple spirits, but this was the first time I had to deal with such raw emotion that spilled out of them. It was when I realized they weren't that different than we are. Of course, that is a hotly contested point."

"What do you mean?", Ralph asked.

"Well, Father Lucian told me until his death, that he believed I was supplanting the emotions I would have felt in those situations onto them. I tended to believe he felt that way because he had never felt that from any of his experiences. Of course, there is nothing scientific about any of this. He could be right," she said, holding up a hand, palm pointed up to the ceiling. "Or I could be," she smirked and raised the other hand. "No one will ever know. It is all perspective. See, much of life is. Very little is black or white. It is mostly shades of gray. It's we who paint the lines."

"Yes, we do, don't we," Ralph said smiling. "Did dismissing, as you have called it before, stop the attacks?"

"I presume so. There were only two known attacks. The actual crime in 1941, and the one against Lauren Middleton. Since our visit, there have been no other issues, or as far as I have heard. Which saddens me a little."

Ralph acted surprised at that answer. He leaned forward and probed, "Why is that? If you don't mind me asking."

"While I removed an entity that had given himself over to dark forces, I also allowed two innocent spirits to find peace. For that I am happy, but I also robbed the world of a good ghost story." A mischievous smile crossed her face.

"I see. They can still tell the story though."

"They can, and I am sure they do. There just aren't any natural, or unnatural, bumps in the night to give those that go looking that little jolt."

The entire room chuckled at that reply. Kenneth stood up from behind the camera to look on the group with his own eyes.

"You took away a ghost story and solved one," he stopped and then corrected himself, "two crimes. I am sure the local law enforcement agencies were happy about that."

"Well, in a way. It conflicted them. They had the answers to both the 1941 murders and the current one, but that presented another and much larger problem.

How to report and document both. They very well couldn't document that a ghost killed Lauren Middleton, now could they?"

"So how did they handle it?"

"The case is still a cold case, just in a different cabinet, so no one will ever go looking again. The same with the 1941 murders of Bette Richeson and Ruth Pickering."

"But they had a name, right?", Ralph questioned. His pad emerged with his handy pencil. Both sat at the ready to make a note.

"Nope. Well, yes, they had a name, or Detective Burrows did, and that is as far as it went. See, I made that man a promise. When he looked up at me and told me he accepted God, I promised to not tear him down."

"So you won't tell us the name?"

# The Stories of Sister Sarah

Crossed

David Clark

# 1

The morning chill of the clear spring morning was now a thing of the past. Clear skies and a strong sun chased it away. It wasn't hot outside. It was pleasant, and a gentle breeze brought in a refreshing respite along with the sweet smell of jasmine and honeysuckle from time to time. There was no questioning why Sister Sarah called this her Eden, it truly was heaven on Earth.

Kenneth may have somewhat disagreed, as he had to search around for the perfect angle to set up to avoid having sunspots and glare during his shot. He tried to work around where the Sister sat, not wanting to ask the elderly nun to move. Though she did shift a little on the bench as he moved around. Ralph assisted by standing in a spot and then calling for Kenneth to bring the camera over there and check. Neither hesitated when Sister Sarah Meyer recommended taking today's sessions outside. It was beautiful and would provide an alternative to the dark wood and stone backdrops they have used over the last few sessions.

After a few moments of searching, Kenneth found the perfect spot and quickly setup. Ralph positioned the footstool he had carried outside with him in front of Sarah. Behind her, as always was one of her escorts, and her brother, Jacob.

"You were right. This is beautiful," Ralph said, motioning at the tree filled courtyard that was all around them.

"It is. This is my sanctuary. No matter what is going on, or how I feel, this is where I come to feel right as rain," Sarah said with a smile. "So, what shall we talk about today?"

"Well," Ralph started. "I was thinking we could talk about the hill."

"Lithuania?", Sarah tersely asked.

"If that is okay?"

Sarah looked around the courtyard and up into the olive tree leaves that blew in the breeze. It appeared she searched for a divine answer. Whether it arrived or not, only Sarah knew. She looked down at her hands in her lap and then up at her brother. There was a single tear dripping down her cheek.

"Sister, we can cover something else today," Ralph said as Jacob handed his sister a handkerchief.

"No, it's okay," she sniffed. "I knew we were going to have to talk about it at some point."

"We can wait," Ralph offered.

Jacob chimed in, "Maybe it is best if we wait."

"No. No. The story has to be told. There is no avoiding it. Let's go ahead." Sarah righted herself and handed the handkerchief back to her brother. She was again the picture of strong, resolute faith. "So, the hill in Lithuania?"

"Yes, Sister. That was what, eight years after you arrived here?"

"Eleven that October," corrected Sarah with a little smirk.

Ralph made a note on his notepad. "A few questions before we get started with what happened."

Sarah nodded her agreement.

"Before Father Lucian came to you, had you heard about the hill?", asked Ralph. He looked on eagerly for her response.

"No. I had never heard of such a place until that day. Since then, I have spent many hours reading up on it. On the surface, it is a fascinating place. A hill, with thousands upon thousands of crosses on it. Quite a sight from the pictures I have seen, and another good example of how the Church is able to control the story. For over a hundred years, everyone knew it as a monument for the struggles of the Lithuania people and the oppression they felt during the World Wars. Which, as we all know now, is somewhat true, but it has nothing to do with either World War I or World War II"

"And, Sister, what was the real purpose?"

"Mind you, a Pope even visited the site to further the hoax," Sarah said with a point and a chuckle.

"The real purpose?", Ralph asked again.

The chuckle and smile vacated Sarah, and she leaned forward with a sternness in her eyes. "It was a spiritual lock to contain a monster, of course."

"Are there any others like it around the world?"

"Of course," Sister Sarah said very matter-of-factly. "But don't ask me where because I won't tell you. Those things need to stay undisturbed." Her head shook from side to side, and she leaned back and crossed her arms.

"Of course not, Sister. I was just curious."

"Oh, I know. Most are, and I do get a sense from you and young Kenneth that neither of you are looking to cause any trouble." This was something Sarah realized about them during her first meeting and knew Jacob had as well, or Jacob would have never agreed to allow them to meet with her. "There is a lot more to this world than meets the eye. Hidden secrets, treasures, and truths all over the place. Take my word for it," she leaned forward and whispered, "everything is better if those stay hidden." Sarah studied Ralph, waiting for him to acknowledge her suggestion. When he did, she added, "We don't need you going out and doing any documentaries on those and have someone who doesn't know any better poking around and unleashing hell on Earth. There are enough of those that should know better doing that as it is, and I and my brother are way too old to fix things."

Next to her, Jacob puffed out his chest a little and drew a wry laugh from his sister. "I am younger than you, remember?"

"Oh, I remember. You are younger than me, but neither of us are spring chickens." She reached over and ran her fingers through his mop of grey hair, which Jacob did the same to straighten anything she had moved out of place. "This younger generation of keepers is a fine bunch and will do all right when dealing with the normal day to day, but there isn't a leader yet. Someone that will step forward when a real challenge appears, not like my brother here." Sarah was proud of her brother, probably more than she had ever really told him. It was part of the sister brother dynamic. She knew they loved each other, and she was immensely proud of him, even though she didn't say it as often as she should have or if ever. This was one of the first times she had ever vocalized it, and it appeared to embarrass Jacob as he broke eye contact with his sister. Similarly, Sarah knew Jacob was proud of her. Sarah kept her loving gaze on her brother.

"I am sorry, dear. I didn't mean to interrupt your questions. Continue," she said, turning back to Ralph.

"No apology needed," Ralph said. "The last question I have before we let you tell us about your experience at the hill, had you met Madame Styvia or Lord Negiev before you arrived in Lithuania?"

"Yes and no. Do I remember meeting them? No. But, they were part of the group of keepers that rescued me in Miller's Crossing and before I came here, which made things interesting. Let me go ahead and tell you my story, you will understand then."

A grouping of dark clouds formed above them, ruining the perfectly clear blue sky, and the refreshing breeze became evil.

# 2

"Dad, I am so sorry," Sarah said. She looked out from the woods as her father, Father Murray, Jacob, Father Lucian, and six strangers approached. Her father couldn't hear her at this distance. But, even if he were closer, he still wouldn't. She was there, but not. She could see the destruction she had caused, but IT wouldn't let her do anything about it except suffer the pure fear and despair that coursed through every fiber of her being like the water of all the worlds' rivers flowing through a garden hose at the same time. There was no way for her to stem the tide of sorrow. Suffer it she must, and death appeared to be her only salvation.

Four rapid knocks at her chamber door interrupted this all too familiar dream. Unfortunately, this interruption didn't happen far too often enough. When she thought about it in the first moments of cognitive thought as sleep lost its grasp on her, while the terror of the nightmare hung on, they had never woken her during the night in the eleven years since her arrival at the Abbey.

She sat up and looked around the room. Her quaint chambers should be completely dark while she slept; that was how Sarah would prefer it. The presence of her nightly tenders made her feel odd about it though, so she always kept a single candle lit on her nightstand. She swung her feet to the floor and oriented herself in the flickering light. It was silent except for the prayer that was a constant companion. It was something that was so much a part of her world it blended into her own existence to the point of not noticing it at all. A few times that caused her to panic and search for that sweet sound, just to make sure it was still there. For just a moment, she wondered if she had heard the knock in her dreams only, and looked at Sister Mary Theresa and asked, "Was there a knock?" The Sister didn't open her eyes when she nodded her head, confirming that the knock had indeed happened. If that wasn't enough of a confirmation, the second set of four rapid knocks was.

The stone floor was cold on Sarah's feet as she walked toward the door. Another round of knocking started, and she opened it between the second and third rap. On the other side was Father Lucian, out of breath and with a concerned look on his face she had never seen before. She didn't even see this much concern when he faced her down in her nightmare.

"Sister," he said with a gasp. "I need you to get dressed and come with me. Right now!"

"Father, what's going on?" Mother Francine asked. She rushed down the hall from her chamber. It was good, she asked. If she hadn't, it would be the next sound that escaped Sarah's mouth.

"It's Šiauliai. There's been an earthquake," he said.

Sarah didn't understand what he was talking about, but it was obvious her Mother Superior did. She stopped dead in her tracks and her hand leapt to her chest. "The seal... is it breached?", she asked.

"Holding, but barely. Everything fell."

Mother Francine rushed past Father Lucian and pushed past Sarah and into her room. "Child, let me help you get ready." Her hand grabbed Sarah's and pulled her inside. Sarah felt a tremble in her touch until she released her to close the door.

"Mother, what is it?"

"We must hurry," she said, and opened the simple bureau and pulled out a habit and placed it on Sarah's bed. "Come Sarah, you must get dressed." She turned to Sister Mary Theresa, who looked on from the corner, but never stopped her prayer. "Sisters Cecilia, Angelica and Genevieve will accompany her. Go get them prepared. I'll handle things here." Sister Mary Theresa stopped, stood up, and walked quickly to the door, and out. Mother Francine took up the position in the corner and began the prayer while Sarah got dressed.

"Mother, what is this place?", Sarah asked, and then attempted to repeat the name of the place she heard Father Lucian say, "Šiauliai?"

Mother Francine shook her head while she continued the prayer, but the look in her eyes said it all. She was scared. When Sarah finished getting dressed, she opened the door. Father Lucian was still outside. Without a word he started down the hall, and Mother Francine joined the pair in the hall and followed them out to the front.

"Father, can you tell me what is going on?", beseeched Sarah.

"Let's get to the car first," he said from the front of the line.

Sarah's escorts were waiting for them outside the front gate. They started praying as soon as she stepped through the gate. Mother Francine stopped. Father Lucian opened the front and back doors of the black SUV that waited for them. Her three escorts stepped into the back, and Father Lucian in the front, as was the normal seating order for all of her excursions out. Just as Sarah went to take her customary window seat in the back, Mother Francine grabbed her and pulled in close for an embrace that was tighter than normal. Quivers spread from her to Sarah, and her voice shook as she told her. "Take care, child. I mean it, be careful." She released her, which was more Sarah pulling away from her as Father Lucian urged her to hurry in. Sarah took her seat and closed the door as the vehicle sped off pressing her into her seat as she struggled to fasten her seat belt.

"Father, will you tell me what is going on?", Sarah asked.

He didn't turn around to look at her. He didn't even turn slightly in her direction. Instead, he stayed rigidly straight, eyes front, as he spoke. "At 10:13 pm local time last night a magnitude 7.2 earthquake hit Lithuania. Its epicenter was about fifteen miles from the small village of Šiauliai. The loss of life is already devastating, but it is nothing like what will occur if we don't intervene."

"There are aid organizations for this. The Red Cross and Red Crescent deal with these kinds of events all the time. What can we do?", Sarah asked. She didn't have a problem going to assist, but had to wonder what the urgency was for their small party to get in motion when thousands upon thousands of disaster aid trained volunteers would already be on the ground by the time they arrived, and why just them? If they were going to help, perhaps the whole convent should go. This didn't feel like one of their normal assignments.

"Sarah," he said and finally turned toward her. "Do you remember what I taught you about seals?"

This was a topic she had to think about to recall. The term was there in her head, but she hadn't heard it since then. It was mixed in with the symbolism of certain signs that one might come across and their meaning beyond what the public believes it to be. Some are warnings to stay away from places or objects, and others are locks meant to keep something sealed deep inside. One lesson came to mind. A picture of a simple tarnished brass doorknob with the cross and papal crossed keys on it. It was pretty, and one someone might picture being on a thousand or more year old door lining the hallways of the Vatican itself. Instead, it was on the door of an old Christian mission in Uganda. Behind the door, was a creature that possessed an entire village, turning its inhabitants against each other until it left no one alive. "The symbols?", she asked.

"Yes. The village of Šiauliai is the location of a hill with a seal on it. Underneath that hill is Ala, the demon of bad weather. But, don't let that name fool you. Yes, when it was loose it sent terrible weather, hail and tornados through crops and farms robbing an entire village of their food supply, starving them. That was just the edge of its power. When it wanted to really demonstrate true power and enslave people, it rained fire down on them, burning everything alive. In 1853 Pope Pius IX spent ninety-four days battling the beast before locking it in a deep hole beneath the ground. When the beast fell into that chasm it pulled the sides down on top of it covering it with earth. Pope Sylvester put a seal on top of the hill it created to lock it inside. The seal was a simple wooden cross planted into the ground. While it may seem small, it was powerful enough to imprison Ala. Through the years, thousands of pilgrims that understand the true meaning of the hill have placed additional ones adding to the security of the seal. Today there are over ten thousand crosses there. The earthquake knocked them all down, weakening the seal. I received a call from the keeper assigned there to watch over the seal that the ground was pulsing."

"Pulsing, Father?", Sarah asked. In her mind was the image of a bump of green grass rising and falling, like it was breathing.

He turned around further and looked Sarah right in the eye. "It knows the seal is gone and it is trying to get out."

# 3

The first light of the new day should have broken over the eastern horizon over an hour ago, but it hadn't. It was still pitch black as they drove into Šiauliai. The sun hadn't forgotten to come up that day. Sarah had seen it from the window of the plane, but it disappeared as they descended into a bank of what she believed to be clouds. They were clouds, but not of a natural variety. These were large rolling dark clouds of smoke and dust from the hundreds of fires burning across the countryside. Some probably fueled by broken gas lines caused by the earthquake, but an uneasiness creeping up her spine told her some were caused by something unnatural.

As they drove into the city, the glow from some of the larger fires helped illuminate the billowing clouds of smoke and back lit the piles of rubble that used to be buildings, business, and homes. The devastation was complete, and groups of people wandered around aimlessly, with their attention elsewhere, while members of the military and emergency services attempted to provide aid wherever they could. The car carrying Father Lucian, Sister Sarah, and her escorts didn't stop. Their destination was northeast of the city which was the direction everyone she had seen was looking.

Father Lucian had instructed the driver to take them to the Hill of Crosses Information Center, a tourist center for the location. It seemed the hill was such an oddity it had become a destination for tourists, which was not all that surprising to Sarah. Knowing there was a place you could go to see the world's largest ball of twine back in the States was proof that they could make any location into a tourist trap. Probably like all places, there would be a place to park, a building with artifacts and displays about the hill, and of course, a gift shop.

The car screeched to a sudden stop when Father Lucian cried out, "Stop right here! Right here!" They were in the middle of nowhere, with no information center in sight, meaning Sarah would have to wait to see if her assumptions were correct.

He opened the door and got out without a word to anyone. Sarah sat inside it and stared out at the foreign landscape from the safety of the car window. If she didn't know better, she would have thought Father Lucian had just brought them to a battlefield of some war between superpowers. Trees laid down all along the road, and in the distance a fire roared. The intensity of it seemed to grow and wane as each rumble below the car hit and disappeared. Sarah hadn't noticed the aftershocks when they were driving, but now that they sat still, the car rocked and rolled on its springs with every rumble.

After the third rumble, Sarah exited the car to search for Father Lucian who had disappeared into the darkness. He hadn't gone far and was just up the road from the car talking to someone. A woman who turned abruptly and scowled when she saw Sarah.

"Father! Why did you bring.. that... that abomination?", said the woman in a thick and harsh eastern European accent that cut at Sarah. The pale skinned woman with flowing raven hair took up an aggressive pose. Almost a crouch, as if ready to spring on a prey that crossed her path, and Sarah felt like that prey. "Don't we have enough to deal with?", she hissed.

Inside, Sarah felt something rumble and twist. This was the first time in years she had felt its presence when she hadn't tapped into it directly. The feeling of fear she felt multiplied, but her flight instinct wasn't close to being triggered. It was her fight instinct that was loading up, and it wasn't all her. It was mostly IT, and she couldn't quell it.

A hand from behind reached up and grabbed her wrist. Sarah looked down at the hand and followed the arm back to Sister Genevieve, who stood close and prayed. The dark brown eyes of the mid-thirties French nun, who had become a close friend of Sarah's, begged her, and Sarah didn't have to ask what it was about. They could all feel IT stirring inside her. She prayed herself and closed her eyes, attempting to calm everything down. She felt it was working until she felt a breath on her face. She opened her eyes and found herself face to face with the woman.

"Father, get her out of here. Now!", said the woman as she stormed off. "I should have killed her when I had the chance. You said you would keep her under control. This is not under control. I feel it inside her, wanting to get out. Wanting to do what IT does best. And she," she said while her arm exploded behind her with a point back at Sarah, "can't stop it if it wants to."

"She has far more control than you give her credit for. Plus, she has help. And, she is our best hope for solving this problem," said Father Lucian.

"Psh. I seriously doubt that," she scoffed.

It added to the buildup Sarah felt growing inside. This time it wasn't her companion, Abaddon, not that she knew of. This was all her. Her pride and stubborn attitude, both she had to fight at times to keep in check at the convent. Here they were about to be on full display.

"Excuse me, but who the hell are you?," Sarah asked as she chased the woman. "I am in complete control of whatever you think I am."

Sarah had barely finished her declaration before the woman turned and leapt at her, covering an unimaginable distance for a human. Her hand gripped around Sarah's throat and lifted her up with a strength that didn't match her feminine frame. "Let's see how much control it allows you to keep while I choke the life out of you."

"Styvia, put her down. Now!", Father Lucian yelled, and he put himself in between the two women. "Now stop it. We are here to deal with that!", he pointed in the hill's direction to remind them as the ground beneath their feet rumbled again.

"Yes, Father," the woman said.

"Sarah, you will need to excuse Madame Styvia. You two have met once. She was one of the keepers that risked her life to rescue you," Father Lucian said to Sarah, and then turned his attention to Madame Styvia. "Styvia, control yourself. If you feel Abaddon, it is not because of Sarah's lack of control. It is because of the proximity of it to Ala. They are from the same hierarchy of demons. She has complete control over it, and the sisters that are here with her are the safety net just in case."

Styvia? The name was strangely familiar to Sarah, but couldn't remember specifics. She didn't remember seeing her before, even though she had just been told she had. How could she not remember seeing a woman that looks like the bride of a vampire himself with her dark hair, and pale white skin? A sadness she hadn't felt in years came back to her. Sarah knew people had been hurt and killed by what had happened. Had she hurt this woman? Maybe she killed someone she loved or knew? That would explain her reaction. This dark scar on Sarah's past was one she tried to cover up with all the good she had done, but no matter what, it always resurfaced and took a toll on her spirit.

"Now, tell me the current situation?", Father Lucian asked Madame Styvia. Behind them was a gathered mass of townsfolk who were not worried about cleaning up the damage done to their town. Instead, they were concerned about what was occurring on the hill.

"The seal is cracked, not broken, yet. But, I can't tell how bad the crack is. I can't get close enough," Madame Styvia reported.

"Why not?", Father Lucian asked and stepped toward the hill himself. The strongest rumble of the ground rolled past them, throwing the car up in the air and into a ditch next to the road. Sarah and her escort landed sprawled out on the tarmac of the road. Father Lucian tumbled and landed on his backside on the road. Madame Styvia had crouched low to the ground and rode the wave.

"That's why," she said.

As the rumble cleared past them, Sarah felt a familiar tingle and a dark and cold presence off in the distance. She had barely felt it on the drive in, but there was no mistaken it was there now, and it was an evil that weighed down on both her body and soul. It pulsated with the glow from the fire on the hill.

"Either it is another quake, a ring of fire that chases us back, or the attacks on your mind. And now, there is some force... just there," she pointed in front of her," I can't get through it. I am trying to do what I can from here to seal any cracks," continued Madame Styvia.

Sarah got up to her feet and took a few steps forward, beyond Father Lucian and Madame Styvia. She held her right hand out and extended both fingers into an area of unseen power at the edge of her reach. It pushed back at her, but Sarah's fingers pierced the barrier for just a moment before it pushed back, sending her tumbling down to her backside. Her hand and arm tingled painfully. "I can feel it."

# 4

"I can too, and even you can't get through," mocked Madame Styvia. "We need to do something fast, and I am not thrilled about doing this in the dark."

Father Lucian strode back to the car and leaned in the passenger seat. From where Sarah stood, she could see he was plundering through his bag. He emerged wearing a red stole, and a familiar crown of thorns. She saw the bible in his hands as he walked past her, and without a word stepped into and through the barrier that had just repulsed her backward to the ground.

"Let's go," he said. His words muffled by a rumble that seemed more like the growl of some great beast below their feet. Even when the peak of the rumble subsided, there was a slight low vibration, re-enforcing the image of a great beast letting out a growl with every exhale. The ground moved up and down just enough to be felt with every sound.

Madame Styvia fell in behind Father Lucian. Both crossed through the barrier with ease. They paused on the other side and waited on Sarah. It was now her turn. Of course, it wouldn't just be her. Sisters Genevieve, Angelica, and Cecelia would need to accompany her in. She felt a dread, not for what was ahead of her, but for what the others were about to go through. She felt the dark and deep hatred of evil that waited at the hill for them. It was there in the air, in the dust, and in everything else around them. Infecting everything and everyone around, sending them further into despair.

"It will be okay," she said to the other sisters, trying to sound like an expert who knew exactly what would happen. Inside, she had no clue what they were all in for other than it wasn't good.

They didn't hesitate or waver. Just as always, the Sisters of San Francesco did their duty and stepped through in a line, one after another. Praying the entire way. Only Sister Genevieve looked up at Sarah as she passed. She was the one sister Sarah had connected with the most since her arrival. They crossed through and joined Father Lucian and Madame Styvia without incident. It was now Sarah's turn.

She had tested the barrier once and pushed into it. Whatever 'it' was, it didn't seem to like her intrusion and threw her back. What it would do now, she didn't know. Had Father Lucian cleared a path? It appeared he had. The others had no problem walking through. She didn't know for sure, but had to trust her faith. Both her faith in Father Lucian, and her own faith.

Each step was timid as she crossed through. There was nothing as she followed the same path as the others. Always being a curious animal, she reached to the side with her left hand and leaned. It was there, just a few feet away. She yanked her hand back as soon as she felt it. Any desire of a repeat of earlier had left her, and she stayed on the straight and narrow path Father Lucian had cleared for her. Much like she had for the last several years.

They walked in single file passed the mangled downed trees, and large patches of Earth thrusted up. Whether they had been done so by natural forces or supernatural, Sarah wasn't sure. It didn't really matter. The entire scene was a display of massive destructive power. She had never seen the area before, but with a village so close she had to imagine it was a beautiful countryside, and not the dystopian scene from one of the lower levels of Hell it was now. It was made even more so with the glowing of fires along the horizon everywhere you looked. The one ahead of them glowed brighter than all the others. The dark red halo grew with every rumble of the ground.

They walked for several minutes toward the hill, with the ground rumbling under their feet. Sarah felt a stomach pain developing. It wasn't much at first. Just the typical pain she had a few times as a child when she ate too much, or had something that didn't agree with her like the time her father tried an Asian recipe he saw on television. She visited the bathroom more than her own bedroom for the next few days after that. This was like that, but also strange as it became more intense, with an occasional stab. And unlike the other pain, where she could feel it isolated to one spot, this seemed to move around inside.

"This way," Madame Styvia said. Her hand pointed off the road to the right. Father Lucian followed her direction and led the line of individuals on to a crushed stone path. When Sarah stepped off the road, a sharp pain hit her like a bolt, and sent her to her knees. She didn't say anything, or groan, but somehow her three escorts knew and had stopped and turned to look at her. Fear dripped from their face.

Sarah got up and took another step. Again, another sharp pain, followed by a tightening and twisting of her stomach. Someone or something was trying to tie it into knots, and from the feeling of it, they had succeeded and were going for a double knot. This didn't send her to the ground, but it wasn't for lack of trying. Sarah toughed through it to try to assure the others she was okay. By the third hit, Father Lucian and Madame Styvia had taken notice.

"I am fine," croaked Sarah. "Just my stomach."

"Are you sure that is it?", Madame Styvia asked with the concern of the iceberg that hit the Titanic.

There was no way Sarah would admit how bad the pain was. Showing any signs of weakness would just give her one more reason not to trust her. Even when

Sister Genevieve reached back for her, Sarah brushed her away, and gutted out three steps to reach the others and a sight that momentarily distracted her from the pain. No one had explained to her what she might see at the Hill of a Thousand Crosses. The image her mind constructed was a large grass cover hill with white crosses running up and down it. Like the memorial in Normandy she had visited once with Father Lucian, on a rather simple matter. What she wouldn't give for something as simple as just sending an old honorable vet to a place he can finally find eternal peace now.

What she saw were crosses of all types, shapes, and sizes lining the path that led them up to an elongated rise in the ground, where there were more crosses. It was astonishing and horrifying to see. Instead of seeing the crosses in the ground, they were floating above the ground, in what Sarah had to assume was not their natural state. The ones closest to them shook as they passed.

"Father, how close do you think we need to be to fix the seal?", Sarah asked. Her voice trembled, as did her hands. Any concern about seeming weak had disappeared. Erased by the fear that had moved in.

"We must be on top of the hill," he said, sounding as stone solid as always.

They continued forward. Sarah forced each step, even though the pain had increased to the point where she had started to pant. The number of crosses around them increased the closer they came to the hill itself. All floating. All shook as they passed. Now they rattled against one another, creating an ear shattering sound that Sarah knew was a warning, like the tail of a rattlesnake. The warning had been heard, but not heeded. A slender set of concrete stairs came into view ahead of them. It led up the hill itself through the sea of floating and rattling wood, stone, and metal crosses. They were no more than ten feet away when it all happened. A pain unlike anything Sarah had felt before sent her to the ground. It was a good thing, too. Several crosses flew at her, slashing through the area she had been standing. If she hadn't fallen, they would have impaled her. Her three escorts dropped next to her to avoid another volley.

Amid the horrifying rattle and crashes of wood, stone, and metal smashing into the surrounding ground, she heard Madame Styvia yelling commands at the crosses as they came past her. She stood her ground and held out a familiar looking cross. A white light blasted forward from it, melting the projectiles on contact. Sarah saw Father Lucian beside the warrior, but something was wrong. He was knelt down on one knee, and his head hung down. Madame Styvia was protecting him. In fact, she was protecting all of them, or trying to. A few crosses still made it through behind her and crossed above Sarah and her escort's heads. After seeing one almost take out Madame Styvia from behind, Sarah forced herself up, but only made it as far as a single knee, with one hand still propped on the ground. The other hand held up behind them. In it, the cross of her own. Not of the sacred wood like the one Madame

Styvia had, just a simple gold cross, but it did what it needed to and focused Sarah's power and shot its own beam of truth out, brighter than that of Madame Styvia, blasting the approaching crosses and continuing on to destroy those floating in the surrounding distance.

The attack stopped, and both Madame Styvia and Sarah put away their crosses. Those that floated around them rose up and exploded down into the ground with a thunderous boom. Each now stood firm in place, upside down upon the holy ground.

Sarah saw Madame Styvia hunched over Father Lucian and crawled up to his side. Her teacher, her rock, her center, knelt there with a simple rusted iron cross through the right side of his chest just below the collar bone. Blood soaked his stole and black coat. The stone solid confidence was gone from his eyes. Mortality had set in, and Sarah could see in them the fear of his own end.

# 5

"Hang with us, Father!", exclaimed Sarah. She cradled his head in the back of the car as they sped down the barren road and back to the burning and half destroyed village. Madame Styvia and Sister Cecelia were in the front.

"Turn here!", directed Madame Styvia. The driver yanked the car to the left, slamming the occupants around. Father Lucian let out a groan. Sarah tried to keep him as still as possible, but there was only so much she could do.

"Two blocks and a right!"

Sarah attempted to brace herself and the Father for the next turn. She did better this time. Using her body as a cushion against the door. One hand cradled his head on her lap, the other hand pressed down on his stole, which was now balled up covering the gushing wound. When the car straightened on the road, Sarah looked up at the surrounding buildings. Large cracks plagued what stone covered front facades not already in piles of rubble on the ground. Every so often there was a building that was nothing more than a pile of rubble now. There were no fires on this road, but plenty of distraught survivors. All watched as they approached and continued to watch as the car passed by them. Sarah had to wonder how much these villagers know of what was really going on out there.

"The third house on the next block... on the right!", barked Madame Styvia.

"We are almost there, Father," Sarah said to Father Lucian. His eyes were closed, and his breathing labored.

The car slammed to a stop, and Madame Styvia exploded out and yanked open the back door. Sarah almost fell out backward, but caught herself. She stepped out, but leaned into the car to keep pressure on Father Lucian's wound.

"We need help!", Madame Styvia yelled toward the dark brown wooden door. It burst open as if her voice had ordered it to do so, and two men in dark suits and black hats rushed outside. One ran around the other side of the car and opened the backdoor on that side. The other came to Sarah's side and placed his hands under the Fathers' shoulders.

"Sister, we are going to lift him. You maintain pressure." the man said in a thick eastern European accent. Sarah backed away from the car while the man lifted and pulled Father Lucian from the backseat. The man on the other side came through the car holding the Father's legs. Once both were out, Sarah placed her blood stained hand back on the stole in an attempt to stop the flow of blood. It was a battle she was losing.

A second car pulled up behind with the other two sisters as Sarah squeezed in through the door with Father Lucian. The inside looked like the inside of any normal home, but the furniture in all three rooms she could see had been pushed to the side clearing the center of the room. Banks of candles and flashlights provided the only illumination. This was now a makeshift field hospital, with bodies lying on sheets on the floor as people ran from one person to the next, tending to them the best they could. Blood-soaked bandages dotted each patient, showing where their injuries were. Moans and screams identified the most severally injured.

"Doctor Johhan. Over here. The Father has been injured!", Madame Styvia screamed.

A man with white sleeves rolled up to his elbows, blood stained skin below that, stood up and rushed toward the group that was now just inside the door. His bearded face bore the stress and weariness of a man with more patients than he could handle. His eyes told Sarah it was not within his nature to try. After a quick look at Father Lucian, he gave a quick direction, "there", pointing to an empty spot in the front room.

Sarah followed the men as they laid Father Lucian down on the spot. Doctor Johhan knelt down and removed the stole, and ripped away Father Lucian's jacket and shirt. Blood pulsated from the gaping hole in Father Lucian's chest. The doctor sprung up and ran through the maze of patients to a table in the other room. There was a rattle of objects on the table, before he turned and rushed back to the Father's side. They positioned two clamps on either end of a severed artery, stopping the loss of blood.

"This is the best I can do. I am not equipped to repair the artery here. He needs a hospital," he said. His hands pinched the wound together and pressed a single suture through the skin from one side. Father Lucian moaned, and his body jerked. "I am sorry, Father. I am out of pain killer," he said, pulling it through and going in for a second pass. He made three complete passes through and then tied it off. "That will hold, but it is all I can do."

"Where is the closest hospital?", Sarah asked.

"It was twenty minutes away, but it was destroyed in the quake. As was the next closest one, Sister." Sarah saw the despair in his eyes. "William!", he called across the room. A boy no more than thirteen ran across to him. His eyes shell shocked. They exchanged words in a language Sarah didn't speak, and then the boy took off through the front door. "I have heard the Red Crescent and military were setting up one at the airport. My son will find out. "

Madame Styvia looked around the rooms. She found another boy, tall and slender. Sarah would guess he was probably sixteen or seventeen. After a few words, he took off out the front door as well. "Gordia will grab William and take the car. It won't take them long to find out."

Sarah and her escorts stayed knelt around Father Lucian, who was still unresponsive. They attempted to stay out of the way, but that was easier said than done in the crowded confines of the room. It wasn't long before she heard cries of, "Sister. Sister!", from across the room. Sarah looked in the voice's direction, but didn't see who had said it. She heard it again, and this time saw an elderly man trying to prop himself up on his elbow as he looked in their direction.

"These are people of strong faith. They want a prayer for their safety," Madame Styvia said to Sarah, her tone toxic and irritating to Sarah. "Can you spare one of them to maybe help these soldiers of Christ?" She pointed to the Sisters.

"Yes," Sarah responded and then told Sister Angelica to go tend to the man. Others began to cry out for them. A few were more seriously injured than the others. Sarah felt it pull at her on the inside. She had been tending to the sick and needy for many years now. "I can help as well."

"You?", shot back Madame Styvia. "You have taken the vows?"

"Yes," Sarah confidently replied, and she showed her the silver ring on her left hand signaling her commitment to the church.

"Blasphemy," spat Madame Styvia. "You are anything but worthy."

"I think you underestimate me and who I am," shot back Sarah. She didn't wait to ask for permission, and summoned Sister Genevieve to come with her as she made her way to the closest person requesting assistance. A woman, not much older than Sarah, laid there with a gash across her forehead and cuts up and down her arms. A homemade splint on her left leg. Hope filled her eyes as she looked up at Sarah.

"Pray with me, Sister," she pleaded in a weak voice.

"Of course, what is your name?", Sarah asked as she placed her hand on the only uninjured area she saw, her shoulder.

"Lillian," she said.

Sarah bowed her head and prayed, "Almighty and Eternal God. You are the everlasting health of those who believe in you. Hear us for Your sick servant Lillian, for who we implore the aid of Your tender mercy, that being restored to physical health, she may give thanks to You. Through Christ, our Lord. Amen."

"Thank you, Sister," the woman said.

"Now rest. Let your faith heal you," Sarah said as she stood up and searched for where to go to next. Doctor Johhan approached her and pointed out a man in the next room, and explained he was close to death. Before he even asked, Sarah knew what the request was. She hadn't given Last Rites before, but knew how, and proceeded to the man.

He was semiconscious while Sarah gave him his Last Rites, and out of compassion, she repeated sections of it to allow him to respond instead of moving on. There was a fear in his eyes, but as she finished, she heard his breathing slow and a look of peace filled his eyes. It stayed there even after his last breath escaped his lungs. She sat peacefully over him for a moment, reflecting before moving to the next. That peace was shattered, as the voice of a man from across the home screamed, "You!" Sarah turned to see a blinding light come at her, and then knock her against the wall of the room, several feet away.

# 6

"What the hell?", Sarah exclaimed. Sister Genevieve rushed to her side, but Sarah motioned her away while she dusted herself off. The hit from whatever it was hurt like nothing she had felt before, but there was something strangely familiar about it. Every head in the room, including those Sarah believed to be unconscious were now looking at one of two people. Her and the man stomping in her direction dressed like a modern day Dracula, putting away a familiar looking cross.

"Why you?," he spewed, marching toward Sarah through the maze of people. He never looked down, but maneuvered through it without a problem. "Don't we have enough to deal with... with that out there? Now you?"

"Marcus!", Styvia screamed, grabbing him just as his hand reached for Sarah's throat. It was inches short as Madame Styvia held him back. He continued to lunge trying to reach Sarah. His fingers stretching and squeezing, until Styvia pushed him back several feet and firmly placed herself between Sarah and the enraged man. A hand still on the vest covered chest of the man. "Father Lucian brought her."

This news didn't seem to settle the man down. He pulled back from Madame Styvia's touch and paced back and forth, leering around at Sarah and mumbling the whole time.

Madame Styvia grabbed him by the shoulders. "I'm not thrilled about it either, but we have bigger problems." She then turned to Sarah, "Don't take this as an approval for you being here. It's not, and for the rest of the time you are here, you are to not go near the hill. Understood?" Before Sarah could answer, she answered for her. "Good."

"Not good enough. I want her out of here. Now!... And... and," he stammered. "That outfit she has on. That is a crime against God."

"What is your problem?", Sarah asked, rather pissed off herself. She felt her temper starting up. This time it was all her.

"See, she doesn't even sound like a nun." The man scoffed at her and then dismissed her with his right hand.

"Sarah Meyer. Meet Lord Marcus Negiev. The keeper responsible for this site, and one that met you in Miller's Crossing."

*Not again.*

"Hi," she said, sounding unsure of herself, and still pissed. With how he reacted to her, she had no doubt something horrible happened. Of course, Sarah didn't know what happened, and Father Lucian refused to tell her ever. He always told her to focus on the future and leave the past behind. Which she found ironic, so much of her life was learning about the past to prepare for the future.

"I assume that thing is still with you," barked Lord Negiev.

"Yes. Always.", replied Sarah.

"Bah. This is stupid," he protested. "I don't care who brought her here. Where is he? We need to talk." The pale man in a black suit and grey vest scanned the room violently.

"Over there." Madame Styvia pointed to Father Lucian lying on the floor with blood soaked bandages covering him.

"Oh my. What happened to him?" Lord Negiev rushed to Father Lucian's side.

"We went to the hill, and it threw crosses at us. He was hit, and severely wounded," Madame Styvia said, pained. "We are trying to find a medical facility we can rush him to. Gordia and William have gone to see if there is a field hospital at the airport. They should be back soon."

"Father. Father. Father. You are going to be okay," Lord Negiev knelt by the unconscious priest and stroked his head. Other than the slow rise and drop of Father Lucian's chest with each breath, he looked lifeless. "This is because of her isn't it?" The care that was in his voice moments ago had drained away, allowing his venom to fill in behind it.

His repeated comments and accusations had created an air of anger in the room, and Sarah was its target. The curious eyes that had looked at her earlier now echoed his rage, darkening the already desperation filled room. She was cornered and didn't like it. Her younger self would have lashed back, but her more mature self just stood there and absorbed it all.

"Stop it!," Madame Styvia shot back at Lord Negiev. "She was there yes, but it was not because of her. It attacked us all. If you want to blame anyone, blame me. I was next to him and missed one."

He let it drop, which didn't surprise Sarah. She knew if she had been the one who missed she would be flying up against the wall again.

"Let's just help who we can while we wait on William and Gordia," Madame Styvia said. "Then, you and I have something to take care of."

"And she will stay here!", Lord Negiev added forcefully.

Sarah waited to see if the other keeper would object, but she didn't and instead moved to help the doctor the best she could. Lord Negiev stayed next to Father Lucian. He spoke to him softly while stroking his forehead with occasional looks at his wound to check the bleeding. Sarah noticed a few of the occasional looks at the wound ended with a glare in her direction.

While the others were doing that, Sarah and Genevieve returned to what they were doing before she was thrown against a wall and sat and prayed with the hurt and suffering. The first few she tended to were hesitant to participate. A remnant of the air of hatred that hung in the room, but after Sarah started that appeared to melt away each time.

The tension that built inside her disappeared as she tended to her duties. It gave her a serenity she had never felt in her life before the convent. To this day, she still remembered the first time she sat with an ill woman and prayed with her in her home in the village of Fiesole. The woman was so caring and accepting, as most Sarah tended to were. And, she wasn't the first Sarah had tended to. Each gave her a feeling of peace, but this one time Sarah could sense the peace and tranquility she gave her. She only paused from her duties when the door opened, as most did to see if there was a new patient to rush and tend to immediately. Sarah wanted to see if the two boys had returned yet with news of the field hospital.

Sarah was growing tired, and concerned, as it had been a while, and many prayers, since the boys left. She had made her way all the way from the front room to two rooms back. From there she could barely hear the opening of the door over the moans and wails. She heard what sounded like the door again, but by the time she looked, it was still closed. She returned to give the man she was tending to, hope; a hope she felt leaving her as the time passed. She wanted to stop what she was doing and go to Father Lucian's side, but not with Lord Negiev there. Nothing could get her that close to that man, and Sarah was pretty sure he wanted it that way too.

# 7

"It is there!" William and Gordia exploded through the door and ran to Doctor Johhan.

"Hold up, William," Gordia cried, out of breath and bent over just inside the door. "It was there. The road is destroyed. Looks like an aftershock took out the airport," he gasped," and everything in it. You can see the tents they set up... all over the ground... mostly on fire."

Doctor Johhan tossed William's hair. "Thanks for trying, William. You too Gordia." He turned to walk back to his patients. To Sarah, he looked to be a man defeated and drained of all hope. He needed that field hospital to be there. Not just for Father Lucian, but for most of the people in the building. This place was nothing more than a place to triage and stabilize, if possible. It wasn't equipped for anything more. The more Sarah thought about it, the more she could relate to how the doctor felt. This was now a place of death, and there was nothing anyone could do to stop it.

Sarah's gaze moved to Father Lucian, and her heart sank the rest of the way into the pit of despair that surrounded her. A tear trickled down her cheek. A second one followed. When the third one attempted to join them, she sniffed and rubbed it away. She needed to be strong. Not for herself. Not for Father Lucian, he wouldn't know the difference in his current state. Not for the other keepers, Sarah didn't really care what they thought of her. It was everyone else. Everyone else that was going to die here and would need comforting. Father Lucian would expect her to do her duty and provide that, and that was what she was going to do.

There was one more gaze in Father Lucian's direction before Sarah went on about her duty. Some final words, and another tear. Madame Styvia and Lord Negiev were doing the same. Both leaned over the Father's body. Sarah knelt down over a woman who, like the Father, was unconscious. Doctor Johhan told her she wouldn't wake up again and wouldn't last the hour. Sarah started a prayer to comfort her soul when, out of the corner of her eye, she saw Madame Styvia and Lord Negiev heading for the door. Sarah stood, still praying.

Everyone not injured or tending to the injured ran to them. They shook their hands, and exchanged hugs and words of luck. Sarah didn't need to be told where they were going and why. The looks both of them gave her told her she wasn't going with them. No matter how much she tried. And just to make sure it was clear, Lord Negiev yelled, "You stay here!". They were out the door.

Sarah thought about running after them, and she wasn't the only one. Sister Genevieve had already started for the door when Sarah stood up. She looked back at Father Lucian laying there, his breathing shallow and labored. He brought her there to do what they were going to do, but they were keepers as well. They were just as capable as she was. The sounds around the rooms reminded her that, she could do something they couldn't, and she knelt back down.

Over the next half hour, they lost more than half of those they attempted to save. Between Sarah and the other sisters, they managed to give each a peaceful passing, which was the best they could do. Sarah wished there was more. During that time, the ground under them rumbled several times. A few small aftershocks, and one large one that brought down large chunks of plaster from the ceiling, adding to the persistent dust cloud that was everywhere you looked. Even from where Sarah was, she could tell the job hadn't been completed. It was still out there.

Doctor Johhan collapsed to the wall and slid to the floor next to Sarah. He was exhausted, and at the moment had no one left that needed treatment. The only victims left had minor cuts and bruises, and a few broken bones, but they were all stable. No one new had come in for hours. Which was also another sad benchmark. It meant there was no one else out there.

Sarah handed him a handkerchief she used to wipe blood and dirt off her hands as she went from person to person. He turned it to a clean side and wiped his forehead. She saw trails through the dust that lined his face telling of the tears he had shed. As his face relaxed, the areas of clean skin in the folds of his brow and the corners of his mouth told of how long his expression had been clinched. His eyes stared at the floor lined with bodies, more covered from head to toe by blankets than not. He had won a few battles today, but Sarah could tell from the tremble in his chin it wasn't enough.

"So why do they hate you?", he asked in a whisper.

That was the question, and Sarah didn't have a good answer, so she gave him the only answer she knew that wouldn't create any additional questions. "We met once before, and it didn't go well."

"It's more than that. I haven't seen Marcus do what he did to you to another person before."

"So, you know what he is?", Sarah asked, unprepared for that.

"A keeper?," he asked. "Yes, most of us do. It's no great secret around here, but we are great at keeping secrets." He pointed in the direction of the hill.

"I guess that's true," Sarah said. Sarah remembered how others in Miller's Crossing knew the truth about their family, even when they didn't. They guarded the secret, much like here. It was probably the same for everyone. A circle of trustees.

"Are you a keeper?"

"Me, no," Sarah said, and then added, "My father and brother are."

"It runs in families, doesn't it?", he asked, sounding more curious than exhausted. Sarah nodded. "Then that makes you a keeper as well. So why did another keeper attack you?"

If the question didn't tell Sarah that Doctor Johhan wasn't letting this go, the fact that he had turned to face her made it loud and clear. She needed a good answer that would satisfy his curiosity. Of course, the moment she needed creativity, the stress, death, and exhaustion she had experienced stifled her ability to come up with anything even believable. Even the truth seemed too out there for most to believe, but knowing he could keep a secret she tried that. "There is a little more to me than you can see. A demon possessed and hasn't let go. It's kept dormant by the prayers performed by the sisters who travel with me."

"A demon?", was his only response.

"Yea, a demon," Sarah said, and noticed a concern and almost fear in his eyes. "Don't worry. It's under control."

"Good," his voice said, still sounding unsure. "Is it safe to assume they had something to do with you and the demon?"

Sarah pressed her face into her hands. She rubbed her eyes, and then massaged her temples before she answered, with her hands still muffling her voice, "They battled the demon to rescue me, or so I have figured out."

"You don't remember?"

"No," Sarah said. "I wish I did, but I don't remember anything but a few slivers here and there. And, those were like watching the most horrifying movie. I have asked, but they won't tell."

"Huh," Doctor Johhan said, and then paused, seemingly lost in thought before he continued. "Good clinical practice there. You don't want to fill in too many details for someone that suffered a severe traumatic event. It could do irreparable psychological harm."

"So, I have been told," Sarah said, wondering if knowing you carried a demon could do similar harm.

"And now? Do you follow Father Lucian around to help as some sort of repentance?", he looked upon Sarah with inquisitive and trusting eyes. She saw no signs of a man afraid of sitting next to a woman possessed by a powerful demon. Why would he? They live with one under their very feet every day. It was refreshing. Sarah always dreaded the day someone found out what she was. The world would fear her as the devil itself. Not here.

"Yes and no. It enhances my abilities and..." a commotion coming through the door interrupted Sarah's explanation, causing both of them to spring to their feet. A cloud of dust rushed in through the door, along with Madame Styvia helping Lord Negiev in. It was obvious to Sarah, their attempt hadn't gone well. The ground growled beneath her feet.

# 8

"What happened?", Sarah asked alarmed.

Madame Styvia helped Lord Negiev down to the floor. He had been roughed up from head to toe. Bruises and cuts covered his body. The neat black suit he left in, was nothing more than tattered cloth now. He landed on the ground with a moan, but was alive and responsive. His hand reached out for Styvia, which she didn't see, and it landed on her leg, but did not grab. It patted her, as if to thank her for dragging him back. "Marcus made a suggestion, that IT did not like," Madame Styvia said, out of breath.

"Ala?", asked Sarah.

What life that was left in Lord Negiev propelled him up to his feet, and he stumbled toward her. Everyone else looked at her stunned. Madame Styvia once again found herself playing peacekeeper, placing herself between Sarah and Marcus. She caught him in her arms and said, "She doesn't know," rather calmly, and helped Marcus back to the ground with the assistance of Doctor Johhan who had already began to examine the torn bits of flesh on Marcus's arms.

"Sister," Madame Styvia turned to Sarah and said, "We don't use the name. Using the name is akin to inviting the demon in."

Just then Sarah remembered her lessons, and the importance of a demon's name. Knowing and speaking a demon's name basically opens a direct line of communication with the creature. It can either invite them in, or cast them out. That is why there is such focus on identifying the demon before taking any action. It helps to know what you are dealing with, and it gives you the true upper hand. "I forgot my lesson. I am sorry."

"It's okay," she said. The tension that existed in her tone earlier was gone. Was it a case she was warming up to Sarah, or worn down by exhaustion? Sarah didn't know. Either way she would take it. "The seal is more than cracked. The ground is showing cracks radiating out from the hill. It won't be long until it finds a weak spot and gets out."

"Father Lucian said," Sarah caught herself about to say the name again, "IT ... was responsible for bad weather. What else can you tell me?"

"Bad weather. If it was only that. It manipulates the forces of nature, so yes, weather, but also fire, ice, floods, you name the natural disaster, and it can summon it. In 1813, it rained over three villages north of here for three solid months, flooding farmlands, drowning livestock, and destroying stored crops. In 1837, there was an eruption sending balls of fire hundreds of miles in all directions. The ensuing wildfires burnt villages to the ground before those living there could get out. In 1848, a flood appeared out of nowhere wiping two villages off the map. None of the hundreds of people that lived in them were ever found. Mind you, there are no rivers in this area that could supply that amount of water, and we are still hundreds of miles from the Baltic Sea. Then in 1850, we were hit by a blizzard, which isn't that out of the ordinary considering where we are, but not in August. The ground stayed frozen until the next spring, killing crops and..."

"I get the picture," interrupted Sarah, "But why? What does it have to gain by destroying farms and villages? Don't demons want something?"

"They do, just not always for themselves," Madame Styvia said. She walked to Sarah, joining her against the wall Sarah sat against having a leisure conversation with Doctor Johhan in the moments before their return. "Remember this is all part of a bigger war. The war of good and evil. The war of God and all else."

"Destruction of faith," they both said together.

"Yes, imagine you are a God-fearing individual. You go to church. You pray and worship. You give of yourself, and what do you receive in return? Destruction. No protection from the very evil the bible says He will protect the penitent from. What I told you were just the large events in the history of this region, but before IT was locked away, there were little things. Single farms, or a couple here and there. Massacres of livestock. Those litter the tales the old timers would tell you. Marcus could tell you a few others. Now I will say after a while everything that goes bad becomes IT's fault. We don't know which of those minor events were truly IT's doing or not, but that should tell you the kind of oppression the people felt with it around."

"Oppression? The cover story? The pope's plaque?", Sarah wondered aloud.

"Makes sense now, doesn't it?"

It sure did. Father Lucian told Sarah the hill of crosses was a monument to the strength of the Lithuanian people and all the oppression they had suffered under the Russians and Germans during the World Wars. It was a monument to the strength and the oppression, and the World Wars gave a good cover story the public would believe, it now all made sense. The constant rumbling of the ground signaled that oppression wanted to return.

"What now?", Sarah asked.

"Well," started Madame Styvia. "We have to go back out there and try to finish this. If you are willing?"

She looked at Sarah with kind eyes, but Sarah remembered her initial reaction and was surprised by the question. "Are you sure you trust me? You didn't seem too happy about seeing me here, and told me I wasn't to go anywhere near the hill."

"Well, you have to remember what Marcus and I went through the first time we met," Sarah started to interrupt, and her hands flew up wildly with her irritation, but Madame Styvia grabbed them, gently. "I know. That was not you, that was him, and I am sure you don't remember anything. Most never do. It was one of the most challenging times as Keepers, and even then, we didn't win. You are more of a stalemate." That term turned the screw a little more inside Sarah. Words were pressing against her lips to get out. "But, Father Lucian trusts you, and he has told us about the work you and he have done. Is it true, your friend's presence enhances your abilities?"

This woman had a way with words, and not in a good way, but Sarah understood the message and the question. Sarah bit her lip. "I wouldn't call him my friend, more of a passenger, and yes, from what I can tell his presence does. I don't need a relic to focus my abilities."

"In that I am jealous, Sister"

"What about him?", Sarah asked looking over at Lord Negiev.

"I wouldn't worry about him. He is in no shape to go back out there, or to stop you and I from going. IT threw tons of pieces of dirt at him, in an attempt to bury him. The sticks and twigs that were in the wave of earth made it through and cut him up pretty good. I think a stone got him in the head too, but he will be okay. I am worried about the Father. We can't get him help until we end this." She looked in the direction of the unconscious Father Lucian. "If we seal IT back up, maybe the quakes will stop and we will have a chance," Madame Styvia said, with a glint in her eye that told Sarah she truly believed that. "Just focus on that, and we can help him."

Sarah looked back at Father Lucian again and watched him. His breathing had become more labored and erratic. Sister Cecelia was still knelt by him and tending to him. She looked up and shook her head, with a grave look on her face. He didn't have long, and Sarah knew it. Something inside her felt him slipping away.

"Shall we?", Madame Styvia asked as if she were asking Sarah to go shopping. She stood up and dusted off her long black dress. Dust and debris had gathered in the ruffles and covered the accents of dark red from her view. A quick shake of her head sent the dust flying from her long raven hair. She headed for the door. Sarah followed with Sister Genevieve.

"No, you can't," cried Lord Negiev as they walked past him. He sat up, reaching toward them.

"Not her. You can't..." he cried again, but those were the last words he screamed before his mind succumbed to the pain rendering him unconscious.

# 9

The clock on the tower in the classic tree-lined walkway and bench littered town square said it was mid-afternoon, but it looked more like late evening. Clouds of smoke and dust still billowed up around them, blocking out the sun, and casting the entire town into a hazy dusk appearance. The landscape was nothing but browns and greys everywhere, like an aged picture. Denser clouds rose from just beyond the horizon, giving it an ominous appearance, like the shadow of a great beast lurking in the haze. If only it wasn't true, but in part it was. And that is why the three women walked toward it.

The use of a car was now out of the question. It appeared in the hours Sarah was inside, other buildings had fallen. Their stone facades were now nothing more than piles of rubble that stretched out into the street. Difficult as it was to climb, they would have been impossible to drive over. Some of the rumbles she had felt were probably the buildings making their last statement in this world before becoming just piles of stone and dust.

"So, that prayer, it's like a seal?", Madame Styvia asked, breaking the silence that had existed between them. Not that Sarah minded the silence. The quiet gave her a moment to think about what was ahead of them, and what to do about it. Her experience to date had been limited to lost spirits and what in the grand scheme of the world were lesser demons. Not that her lessons at the Vatican didn't cover this. But reading stories and recounts of events that happened centuries ago didn't replace practical experience.

"Yea, I guess it is," Sarah agreed. She hadn't thought about it that way before, but it was a type of seal. One placed on her by the other sisters. One that required constant maintenance, care, and feeding by the prayer. "The prayer keeps it in place and maintains its strength. Was there something similar on the hill?", asked Sarah, but then she answered her own question. "The crosses?"

"Yes, the crosses," Madame Sylvia said. "Every week a pilgrimage is made to the hill. They anoint the cross with oil and then dip the bottom spike in holy water before plunging into the ground."

Sarah thought about that for a moment. *Could it be that simple?* It was hard to believe. There may be no need for a battle with this beast, just another cross to lock it back in. With a ton of hope, she asked, "Then we just need to do that again to lock it back."

"Yes, that is true," Madame Styvia answered, straining as she crawled up an enormous pile of debris that blocked the road out of town. It was a combination of mangled buildings, cars, trees, and chunks of ground.

Sarah thought back to her own experiences again. She had discounted them before, but may have been quick to do so. Each was formidable in their own right. But what made them a challenge was not the challenge here. She knew exactly what needed to happen. There was no great mystery to unravel, secret to find, or truth to uncover. This was just a simple, go take that hill, and plunge a cross into the heart of the hill.

From the top of the mound, Madame Styvia stood tall and looked down at Sarah and Sister Genevieve as they climbed up. "Of course, the challenge is even getting close enough to be able to do that." A fact that the true gravity of didn't hit Sarah until she joined Styvia at the top of the mound and looked out at the landscape ahead of them.

Every time Sarah thought she had seen hell on Earth, hell upped its game, but none of them held a candle to this sight. The fire and brimstone of Hades' front porch would have been a vacation spot compared to this. The ground wasn't cracked, it was shattered. Flames roared up through the ruptures as if they were the exhales of the beast underneath. Smoke hovered just above the ground to capture the glow of the flames underneath and letting no light from above through. It smelled of a noxious sulfur. Sarah gasped at the sight.

"Bad, huh?", Madame Styvia asked as she stepped down the pile of rubble.

"I have never seen anything so...", Sarah started, but couldn't find the right word that matched what her eyes saw.

"I did once, it was worse."

Sarah followed her down the pile. Being careful with every step not to land on a loose piece that would slip underneath her. It wasn't the easiest of tasks, but she managed, and every few steps she turned around to make sure Sister Genevieve was doing okay. The sister appeared to be following Sarah's exact steps down the pile. Her attention was down at the rubble, but she kept up her duty.

"It was when we came for you," Madame Styvia said.

She was at the bottom waiting on them, looking straight up at Sarah when she said it. Her look didn't tell Sarah if she was just making an observation or if there was something more behind it. It was business like, as was her tone. Which Sarah understood. Knowing where they were heading had forced her focus on the task at hand. She hadn't even thought about Father Lucian since they left, but she felt there was something there she needed to clear out of the air. "Look, I am not sure what happened back then. No one had told me. I am sorry for whatever it was."

"I know. It's just, this reminds me of that moment," Madame Styvia said. "But then there were more of us. Are you sure of your abilities?"

Sarah proceeded down the pile and once at the bottom she said, "Yes, very." She wasn't, not compared to what they had to deal with, but there wasn't a chance in hell she was going to admit that. Madame Styvia had finally stopped looking at her with contempt, Sarah wasn't about to give her a reason to start again.

"Are you sure that thing is under control?"

"That I am sure of. It hasn't been out since you last saw me," Sarah answered. This answer was the complete truth, and she looked Madame Styvia right in the eyes as she delivered it.

"Just needed to be sure. Let's go."

Sarah helped Sister Genevieve down off the pile, and the three women walked across the broken landscape into the mouth of hell itself. The smell was horrible and burned Sarah's nose, but the heat was the worst. It was oppressive, and Sarah was sweating up a storm in her habit, so much so she removed her headpiece and balled it up in her hand, but not before rolling up the sleeves of her tunic. Her comment to Sister Genevieve, "Not a word to Mother," drew a half-hearted laugh from Madame Styvia. Though it wasn't more than a few moments before she rolled up her sleeves as well.

Sister Genevieve kept her prayer up and showed no distress from the crucible they traveled through, but Sarah knew she was hot and miserable as well, and also knew her well enough to know she wouldn't discard any portions of her habit for comfort. Her faith, duty, and position were above her own comfort, and Sarah knew not to push that too far. But that didn't stop Sarah from reaching over and pushing up the sleeves of her wool garment. It was something Sarah knew the sister wouldn't have done on her own.

They worked through the maze of explosions of flame and smoke. Small patches of earth blasted skyward with each. A few particles of dirt rained down on them as they walked, or tried to. The ground had a constant rumble that grew more intense the closer they came to the hill. Like a wild animal's warning that became louder the closer you got to it. Sarah knew it was only a matter of time before this animal snapped at them and tried to bite. The bark was terrifying, and she had a feeling this was not one of those occasions when the bark was worse than the bite.

# 10

When the Hill came into view, it didn't resemble the place Sarah had seen that morning. It didn't resemble a hill at all. It was a piece of earth that rose and fell with every breath of the great beast. A dark blood red hue bathed the world around them, and waves of heat radiated up from the ground.

As they got closer, the rumble, the growl of the beast, turned into a laugh. Sarah noticed Madame Styvia had removed the cross from around her neck and held it firmly in her hand in front of her. Sarah did the same and spoke a quick blessing. "Lord, watch over us as we spread your righteousness to this foul beast. Give us the strength to overcome the evil with in. Give us the guidance to do what is needed to protect all of your servants from it. In God's name. Amen." There was a quick flash from both of the crosses and Madame Styvia looked at Sarah surprised, but said nothing.

They pushed on to the edge of the crosses. Again, this was a place Sarah believed she stood earlier, but nothing looked familiar. Gone was the worn path created by the hundreds upon thousands of pilgrims that visited the site every year. Also gone were the stairs that lead you up the slight rise to the top of the hill. All that remained were the thousands of crosses stuck upside down in the massive heaving spot of ground.

Sarah heard the deep rumbling laugh again, and said, "We amuse it."

"Yep, but I am not amused." Madame Styvia marched off the path and grabbed the first cross she came to and yanked it up. The ground heaved and screamed, and fought to keep its hold of the object. She pulled back with all her might and the ground lost the battle, giving up the object and sent her falling to the ground with a thud, but with the iron cross in her hand. "Cover me," she yelled, as the ground jerked and shook violently.

Sarah managed to keep her feet, but Sister Genevieve fell to the ground. Sarah positioned herself over her fellow sister and kept her head on a swivel, looking from anything and everything. "What is going to happen?", she exclaimed.

"This is when the storm of dirt hit Marcus before. I just need a few minutes."

During one of the quick spins of her head, Sarah saw Madame Styvia pull out a vial from a pocket. She knew immediately what she was doing and directed Sister Genevieve to slide closer to the other keeper so she could cover them both. She paused her protective scan long enough to watch Madame Styvia expertly anoint the cross in oil and then drip three drops of holy water on the bottom of the ornamental iron cross. One drop ran down it and dripped on the ground. A column of steam exploded upward from the ground, knocking all three women backward. Sarah felt the great rush of steam on her face, but was merely made uncomfortable, not burned. The same for Sister Genevieve. Madame Styvia wasn't so lucky. The scalding jet caught both hands, and her left cheek. She fell to the ground, and appeared to scream, her injured hands held out, but Sarah couldn't hear the scream. The howling that came from all around them drowned out the injured woman's painful wails.

Sister Genevieve moved to help Madame Styvia, and Sarah stood guard over the top of both of them. She expected anything, crosses, sticks, or rocks to come flying at them, and didn't wait to start reciting the various prayers that had served her well through the years. Some were prayers for the sick and dying. Others for traditional prayers to praise her Lord and Savior, but others were of a more personal nature. Ones that she had written and brought with her. Maybe that is why those were the ones she felt a deeper personal connection with. Around them the ground started to glow a bright white, not the dark blood red it had been, and it was quiet. There was no rumble. She could see the waves of the rumble in the surrounding ground approach, but stop at the edge for the ring of light. She continued to pray, and the ring expanded.

"I claim this space in your name," she said, concluding one of her personal prayers, and was about to start another one when she spotted something in the distance approaching them. It was the shadow of a creature that moved on all fours, like an animal. She blinked a few times to clear her vision of the tears caused by the heat and the putrid smell; hoping to see a deer or lost bear that hadn't run off when the earthquake hit. It wasn't an animal, or not at least one she recognized. The proportions of its shape were all wrong. The back legs were twice as long as the front, and had a short but slender frame. The back legs remained stiff with each step. Only the front appeared to bend. With the heat around, Sarah considered the possibility that it was an optical illusion. Like a mirage of water on the road on a hot and sunny day. The appearance of five more of those creatures dismissed that theory.

"Are you able to finish it?", Sarah asked with her voice shaking.

"I will try," Madame Styvia painfully responded.

"Okay, you might want to hurry."

"My hands are," Madame Styvia started. "What are those?"

It was clear to Sarah that she had seen what was now approaching them. "I don't know. Hurry. Please." Sarah took a sideways step to place herself firmly between the shadows and Styvia and Sister Genevieve. The first one was coming close enough to show itself. Now she could see why she thought it was a shadow. Its skin, if the leathery and scaled covered tissue she saw could be called skin, was the blackest black she had ever seen. So black, the light created by the flames didn't reflect off of them. They were just voids in the world. Two yellow eyes were on top of what she had to assume was its head. Short front legs resembled arms, but they didn't use them as such. They were short with a knee or elbow halfway up its length. Its movements appeared to consist of the front appendage reaching forward and clawing a hold in the ground, then its two long stick legs stumbled behind it. Not graceful, but she saw the potential for speed as one of them leapt forward and joined the others, covering a great distance in a single move.

Sarah started reciting her prayers again. And again, a ring of light surrounded them. Sarah's eyes closed, and she concentrated. Her hand reached up and gripped her cross. Feeling the shape of it was something that brought her comfort. Something she first experienced in feeling the worn wood of the relic entrusted to her family. This one was different. Simple and gold, but it worked the same. At first she thought it was just psychological, and then she considered the power of her faith. By accident she found something else though. She didn't need it to focus her abilities to sense or deal with spirits, but occasionally it did give her a boost, and it did again, sending the ring of light out from them a great distance. It seemed to clear the surrounding air this time, too. The putrid odor was gone, as was the smoke and heat. It was pleasant and a little chilly.

The creatures approached the edge of the ring. Sarah watched them intently as they stopped just short of the illuminated ground. She had seen this before and knew they wouldn't step foot inside. If they did, it would kill them. That was what had happened every time in the past. That was why seeing one finally step in, and not screech in pain or dissipate, sent Sarah gasping in fear.

After the first, the second followed, then the third, and finally all of them were again walking toward them, and getting closer, too close. The creatures didn't scream. They didn't howl. From Sarah's vantage point, she wasn't sure they had mouths. All she was sure of, they had sharp claws which were evident with each step.

"How much longer?", Sarah hastily asked.

"Not much."

Sarah looked back behind her at Madame Styvia who had cleaned off the large metal cross and once again was anointing it. Each movement told of the pain she felt in her hands as the oil stung her burns. Next was the holy water, and again Madame Styvia opened the vial and dropped three drops on the cross. This time she used the long skirt of her dress to cradle the cross to keep any drops from rolling off to the ground.

Sarah turned back around and found herself looking eye to eye with two yellow orbs in a sea of nothingness. The creature, not more than a foot away from her, appeared to study her, and still didn't make a sound. Sarah shrieked, making enough noise for everyone. The other creatures had fanned out and surrounded the three of them, but each had their attention on Sarah. Who had sucked the last of her shriek back in and was frantically rubbing at her cross, looking for just a bit of that comfort that it had provided her in the past.

Behind her, Madame Styvia had started a Latin prayer. Sarah heard her voice, but her attention was too focused on their visitors to hear the words. She watched its yellow eyes move from her to Madame Styvia who now held the cross up high above her head. In a single and violent move the creature slapped Sarah aside with its front legs, sending her crashing into another of the creatures which kicked her away with its metal rod like back leg. The pain was excruciating, but the image of all six creatures closing in on Madame Styvia with the cross up in the air, and Sister Genevieve, eyes closed and praying, gave her what she needed to spring up. In that single move, Sarah yanked her cross off her neck and made contact with the closest of the creatures. It shivered and shook and then disappeared. The ground rumbled as it did; the other creatures turned to her. For two of them, they turned too late. Sarah had already dismissed them. Another took a swipe at her from behind, and she ducked and slid under it, using the cross to slash at its otherworldly black skin. The creature fell flat on the ground before it disappeared.

This left two, which watched Sarah intently. They were now the prey, and they knew it. One backed away and moved for Madame Styvia, kicking her in the head with its back leg. The cross Madame Styvia had prepared flew up in the air. Sarah saw it and knew she had to finish this. She went to catch it, slashing a creature on the way. She didn't turn to watch its demise, her focus was the cross. It was also the focus of the remaining creature. The beast knew what it was and was there to stop it. Growing up in a household obsessed with baseball meant that at some point she would be shagging flies for her father or brother. Not because she was asked, but it was just something the whole family did together. Her father would pitch, Jacob would bat, and she was retrieving the balls. She knew to plan for the object she was chasing to drift a little further than it looked and overran where she thought it would land. Her left foot planted hard on the ground to stop her and gave her a powerful stance to lunge forward two steps to intercept the cross before the creature had its chance. She caught it, mid leap, and quickly oriented it with the spike down. As she came down, the creature was under her, making attempts to knock it from her grasp. Sarah held on firmly as she planted it deep in the ground and threw the slender body of the creature.

It disappeared, but Hell appeared. The ground under them swelled up like a balloon. Waves of heat blasted past them. Then on top of the hill, the ground broke, and fire blasted skyward thousands of feet. Sarah rushed to Sister Genevieve who was now helping the unconscious Madame Styvia. Sarah had finished what she had started, but this didn't look like a victory. She helped Sister Genevieve gather her up, and the two women carried the unconscious woman out of danger and back to the small village. The whole way, Sarah wondered, "What do we do now?"

# 11

The journey back was an adventure Sarah wanted to quickly forget. Not only were she and Sister Genevieve carrying the in-and-out-of-consciousness Madame Styvia, they were surrounded by a world intent on killing them. The ground heaved around them with every step. Waves of heat and fire rushed at them. What buildings were left standing above the ground crumbled as they approached, and the debris appeared to be thrown in their direction. All while a continuous roar echoed from behind them. Their only protection was from the aura that radiated out from Sarah. How strong it was, surprised her. It even held a few times when she stopped praying. Every time in the past it had disappeared as soon as the words stopped, whether they were spoken or just in her head. It was as if something deep inside her was helping this time.

Doctor Johhan grabbed Madame Styvia as soon as they collapsed in through the door. Both Sarah and Sister Genevieve fell to their knees. Sarah felt like the weight of the world was off of her shoulders when the doctor and two other men took Madame Styvia, though she wouldn't doubt part of the relief she felt was she could now drop her guard. The sheer adrenaline of the attack at the hill had worn off some time ago, leaving her drained. Sister Angelica came over and checked on both of them. Both women tried to brush her off, but her concern didn't let her give in. She took up the duty while helping Sister Genevieve up before guiding her to a corner and forcing her to sit and let others tend to the scratches that covered her arms and face. Sarah hadn't even noticed them on her until that moment. There was no doubt Sarah was scratched and cut up too. The constant flashes of heat they faced out there had every inch of exposed skin feeling raw, covering the pain from any particular gash.

Sarah wanted to sit down herself and rest, and knew she would, just not here, and forced herself to get up and walk across the room where she finally sprawled out along the side of Father Lucian; every muscle hurt, and she needed to release all the tension in her legs. Sister Cecelia sat on her knees tending to the Father. The look on her face told Sarah everything she needed to know about his condition. Tears had formed in the steadfast nun, though she never let them roll down her cheeks. Always wiping them away before they had a chance. Her cherub face that was known to bring smiles from all who saw her, now waved the flag of defeat. There was no smile, no glow, and no confidence. Sarah thought for a moment he had already passed, but a quick check caught the sight of his chest rising and then falling. What was worrisome is the pace of each breath had slowed down to a pace Sarah didn't know could support life, and each exhale sounded raspy. Fluid, probably blood, was now pooling in his lungs. There had to be a way to get him to help.

Sarah attempted to stand to go talk to several of the men who were helping Doctor Johhan tend to all the patients. She wanted to know if there were any options, no matter how remote. A large rumble along the ground, stronger than the regular growl that had occurred all day long, knocked her back to the ground. The flashlights in the room flickered and then shut off completely, leaving only the light of a few candles to illuminate the space. A strange silence crept in with the darkness. The rumbles, or growls, were gone. Both had been a constant since the quake. No wind outside, or crackling of the fires in the distance. Just the uneasy feeling of nothing. That was when Sarah realized she didn't hear breathing. Hers, Sister Cecelia's who was just across from her, or Father Lucian's. She looked down and saw his chest rise and fall, but there was no raspy sound as the air traveled through fluid and mucus in his lungs. Just behind Sister Cecelia, a woman adjusted a blanket that laid over an injured man. The blanket was large, and the woman stood up to shake it quickly to stretch it out. There was no sound from the material. She had been somewhere like this before. She didn't like it then, and didn't like it now.

Sarah stood up quickly, looking around the room. Her quick moves didn't draw anyone's attention besides Sisters Cecelia and Angelica, who were staring right at her. Sister Angelica stood next to Sarah, her mouth was still moving, but Sarah couldn't hear the constant prayer. Not that that hadn't happened before. It had become so much a fabric of her life, the sound of it had often blended into where she no longer noticed, but this wasn't one of those times. When she tried to hear it, it wasn't there. A parade of pin pricks moved up her spine.

A few others appeared to have taken notice of what was, or wasn't happening. They looked confused and scared, as they tried to talk to each other, but couldn't hear one another. If Sarah knew how to comfort them, it wouldn't make any difference, they wouldn't be able to hear her. A few became frantic and slammed their fist into the floor. There was no bang or thud from the impact, but it did vibrate the table they were close to, causing the light of the candle to flicker ever so slightly, spreading its light outward and into a darkened corner. It was during one of these flickers when Sarah saw it. A shadow whose source was not from the room. It was human, and not human. It stood upright on long muscular legs. Its torso towered up to the ceiling with long arms that dangled down. The face was just a shadow, no features. No eyes. No mouth.

Sarah watched the spot each time the light flickered back into the corner, hoping that her mind was messing with her under the strain of the day. No such luck. It was there each and every time, and it was moving. Each move of the flame showed it had moved several feet in. Its first stop was Lord Negiev, where it appeared to stop right on his chest. Lord Negiev gasped for air. Then there was the kick to Madame Styvia as it passed her. She rolled to the floor, clutching her ribs. Now it was in the light of all the candles and drew the attention of everyone in the room. Most let out silent screams. As it moved passed those screaming, they froze like some a statue in tribute to the horror they felt. Once far enough past, the silent screaming began again. Sarah felt its strange hold grabbing hold of her as it approached. First it was hard to move, then impossible as some invisible force squeezed her. It wasn't painful, but just enough to restrict her movement. Internally she struggled to move, but externally nothing moved.

The shadow leaned down over Father Lucian. It spoke in a deep thunderous voice, and Sarah could hear it. It appeared everyone else could too. The words were not ones she recognized. Powerless, she could only stand there and watched Father Lucian's head rise toward the creature. There was no struggle from the dying priest. All the fight in him had left hours ago. All he had left to offer was his last breath, which he exhaled as a white mist that the shadow appeared to breathe in and lean back to let it soak in.

Emotions flooded inside Sarah from everywhere. Her mentor, her confidant, the man that saved her life and kept her going was now dead at the hands of this beast. Her sorrow mourned his loss. Her sadness knew she would miss their talks. Her compassion worried if he felt pain in his last moments. Her rage wanted revenge. That was a new one. Rage was one emotion she had never felt before, not even as a disgruntled teenager. She had gotten angry a few times. Mad more than a few. She wanted blood this time, and the desire continued to boil inside of her. A finger moved, then a hand. The force that held her was still there, but it was loosening its hold on her. Her arm broke free and she thrust her hand at the shadow. All the rage inside her focused through her hand in a blinding light that sent the shadow flying back through and over people until it came to a stop.

Rage consumed her, and now her legs were free and moving on their own following the creature. It had sprung back up to its feet, looking straight at Sarah. Backing up a few steps it boomed, "You!" Then let out a scream of its own and vanished. Taking with it the veil of silence that had draped over the room. The screams that were silent now filled the room. There was crying and moaning. But one sound was missing. Father Lucian was now silent. There were no more raspy breaths. No rise and fall of his chest. He was gone.

# 12

"It was him!", Madame Styvia cried, still clutching her ribs.

With the return of sound, Sarah's calm returned, and the rage disappeared like fog burning off from her courtyard on a spring day. With it, a flood of questions replaced the dark and dangerous emotion. On top of the list was, "Why did he come here?"

"No!", Madame Styvia exclaimed, struggling to stand. The nurse who had been tending to her burnt hands tried to keep her seated on the ground, but Madame Styvia pushed against her until she was finally on her feet, forcing the woman to follow her up as she wrapped her hands. "I mean, yes. The shadow was behind it. But, what you did, it was him. That thing in you. I felt it as clear as I did that day in the woods," she declared. She paused. Confusion replaced the fear and anger that were both clear on her face. "And, IT was scared of him," she said, puzzled.

"Sister!", exclaimed Sister Genevieve as she ran across the room to Sarah. "I felt him too. That was him."

"That can't be," Madame Styvia questioned out loud. Sarah could see her mind fluttering around as though. It was probably the same thought Sarah had. Each time she or any of the other keepers went out there, they were sent running for their lives. They were no match for Ala and stood no chance of ever re-closing the seal. But her little friend Abaddon seemed to be something Ala wasn't too fond of. *Why?* Well, Sarah remembered there was a hierarchy to demons. A rank, so to speak, just as there is anywhere else in life. In its simplest view, we have the food chain that is based on survival abilities between hunters and preys. Militaries have a chain of command based on responsibility. The demon order is based on influence and ability. Or that is what Sarah remembered being taught by Father Lucian. He gave her a caveat, though. While he believed there was some order based on respect, and possibly fear, in that world, the order they had documented was created by man and should in no way be considered the rule of law. It was a good thing too. She didn't remember the specifics to know where either sat on that tree. The only true evidence she could go on is what she had just seen. Her little friend was higher than Ala.

"Can you control him?", Madame Styvia asked. She again was pushing away from the nurse who had finished wrapping one hand and was attempting to start on the other.

"Yes. No. I don't know," Sarah stammered wearily. Only a few times had she felt a little part of him influencing her and her ability, but that was far different from letting him out and giving him the wheel. She had never even let him out of the trunk before, and the sisters helped her keep both hands on the wheel and both feet on the pedals.

"She can," stated Sister Genevieve. "She has done it before. I have seen her."

"Yea, but not fully. I have let just a bit of him out here and there," protested Sarah. She looked at Madame Styvia, "And, only when absolutely necessary." She looked down at the lifeless body of her mentor and sighed remorsefully. "Father Lucian and one of the sisters have been with me to keep him from taking too much control each time." Her voice sounded almost as lifeless as Father Lucian was. Sarah knew where this was going, and it scared her to death. It meant to open up to what she had feared most since that day. Not just letting Abaddon's presence enhance her abilities, but truly letting him out. Could she hold on to the leash enough to pulling him back when she was ready? She had more than a few doubts.

# 13

*How did I get talked into this?*

Sarah had plenty of time to wonder that as she walked alone back out to the hill. There wasn't much debate about the idea. Sarah didn't even put up a protest; half expecting others to do that for her, but found herself surprised when they didn't. Were they so out of options that the threat of losing her to the demon within was... tolerable?

That thought made her sick to her stomach. This was basically a sacrifice. Send the possessed girl out to face certain death, and hope she can fix the seal before she is lost. Hollywood couldn't come up with a storyline like this. She would laugh, if she didn't feel so scared and, off. The fear was there, but there was something else she couldn't put her finger on. The thought it was him already bubbling up added to her fear and the uneasiness that had a hold on her. This was the first time in years she had been alone with her thoughts. All the time a sister was by her side praying, supporting her, comforting her. She had forgotten what it was like to truly be alone, and she didn't like it.

The ground rumbled around her, but not under her. The flames shooting up from the cracks in the ground in her path stopped. Even the sky above her looked less ominous, changing from a glowing red and black mixture of clouds and fire to grey with every step. Each step she moved deeper and deeper into the grey, feeling less of the world around her. Ahead of her, she saw the hill. She was close. Close enough to see the shadow figure standing on top. *Ala is out*, she thought to herself.

"Yes, he is. The seal of man is broken," said a familiar voice from inside her.

"Oh God," she croaked.

"No my child, God is not here," Abaddon said, and Sarah descended into the grey void.

"Our Father, who art in heaven...", she started. Her voice quivering and echoing in her own head.

"Relax. This is about Ala, not you at the moment."

Sarah felt him getting stronger. The sensation of her life draining away to nothing but a whisper while something else was in control, was one she hoped to never feel again, but here she was. A floating presence along for the ride. The world was just shadows that moved in and out of the static filled void. She could see the shape of the hill and another shape flying at them. It appeared to hit them and knock them to the ground, but she felt no pain. She didn't before either.

They leapt off the ground toward the shadow figure on the hill, covering a great distance and going over the top of Ala. Her hand reached out and scratched gouges into the shadow. Lightning flashed with each slash, and red streaks ran down from the wound as smoke rose from the gashes. It screamed. Her hand made another lightning accented slash from behind, producing another large rip in Ala's black scaley tissue, but they didn't get away unscathed. Its hand reached out and grabbed Sarah, Abaddon, by her long black hair and slung them across the landscape. When they landed, her hands scratched at the ground, trying to grab a hold of something. She finally latched hold of a boulder that had been heaved up by the earthquake, jerking them to a stop just in time. Her legs dangled over the edge of one of the huge cracks in between blasts of flames.

They got up just before the next shot of fire would have consumed them. The heat from the blast singed the ends of Sarah's hair that flowed behind her in the wind, but that didn't stop them. They rushed Ala again. Sarah could only watch as this time her body aimed low for the legs of the towering beast. They hit with a great force, sending the creature stumbling back. They continued to push, forcing it to slide back along the ground. Through the grey void Sarah saw what Abaddon was trying to do. There was a huge rip in the earth's surface at the top of the hill. That was where it was imprisoned. He was trying to put him back. If she could help push she would have, but instead was just along for the ride.

Closer and closer they pushed the creature who struggled for his balance. The flames that had started from the gashes on the top of its shoulder had now grown to cover most of its back. Even though Sarah couldn't hear its screams, she could see its pain. They were almost to the hole when Ala took notice as the back of its foot cleared the edge of the rupture. It grabbed them again by the hair and flipped them up and over its back and down the backside of the hill.

*This isn't working,* Sarah thought. Abaddon had started another attack. Again, focusing on the creature's legs. Ala was ready this time, hunched down in a power stance, legs bent, ready to take the impact. It swiped twice with its hands, contacting the second, swatting them away like a fly. The grey static shook with that impact, giving Sarah a clearer view of the world around them. Ala felt it had the upper hand and again was hurling rocks and chucks of dirt at them. With ninja like quickness, Abaddon dodged every rock, tree, and lump of dirt. Only a volley of iron crosses made it through, slashing at Sarah's skin. None of them were mortal wounds, and for that moment Sarah was appreciative for being in the blank void away from the pain.

Abaddon was slow to get back on his feet. The acts were taking a toll on a level Sarah couldn't understand. Each of these swipes, hits, and slashes were more than they appeared. This was not just two mortals fighting. These were immortals, and each attack delivered an impact from the ages. More of the world crept in as Ala stomped toward them. Looking larger than it had ever looked before.

"You're losing," Sarah exclaimed.

"Shut it. I know what I am doing," Abaddon's voice boomed in the world of static.

"So, you know you are losing," Sarah responded as they made another attack. This time with one of the crosses that Ala had thrown at them. Abaddon grabbed it and ran at the charging Ala, holding it like a spear. He didn't throw it and instead waited until he was on top of him to thrust it at any exposed body part of the creature. The black scaly flesh of Ala bent, but didn't break. The cross did, with a long metallic chink as it broke in two and fell to the ground. Sarah could only watch as the long black clawed hand of their adversary whacked them enough force to send them flying again. Before they even landed, she heard a deep laugh.

"So, you think we are losing?", Abaddon chuckled. "Watch this. I am the great deceiver, remember. I am playing with Ala."

They landed between two rips in the earth's crust. The fire that avoided them now roared up all around them. Through the grey void Sarah saw Ala standing tall. Almost... gloating. *You sick bastard*, was the thought in her head when Abaddon reached out with both of her hands and summoned the flames that roared around them. They leaned toward them and away from their source, towering hundreds of feet in the air, spinning like giant tornadoes. More flames joined them, then dirt, rock, remains of the trees that had been destroyed by the earthquake and Ala. It all mixed into a tower of molten death that was fired at Ala with alarming speed. Even in the void Sarah heard the impact as it exploded on contact, covering him in flames and burning debris, sending him stumbling backwards one step, then a second. The third step was what Abaddon waited for, and Sarah heard the cheer inside when the great creature fell back into the large hole it came from.

"Now I need your help," Abaddon said.

"What?", Sarah asked, surprised. What did he need from her?

"We can't die, and unless you want us to go on fighting forever, which is fine by me, you need to do something. I can't. That is not my thing, and you saw what happened when I tried to use that cross, it broke."

*The yin and the yang*, Sarah thought. They are chaos and she is order. It is up to her to restore order. Confused as to why Abaddon would give her this opening. Why not continue to fight and maybe enslave Ala? Not that she wanted to give him any ideas. It was an opening, and she had to take it. "Then you need to let me out and go back to your spot, don't you?"

"Nice try," he said with his evil laugh. Sarah hoped he would choke on that laugh one day, but she knew there wasn't a chance that would happen. "You get just a little. Just enough to do this." The static cleared more, and Sarah not only could see the world, but could also hear the groaning of the great beast coming from the hole, feel the ground still rumbling under her feet, smell the acidic and toxic sulfur filled fires all around them, and feel the pelting of rain. What she couldn't do is move her own feet. He was still in control of that.

Before Sarah left, Madame Styvia explained the rite to her. It seemed simple enough. Sprinkle some holy water on a series of crosses and plunge them into the ground while proclaiming, "With the power of almighty God, I lock this unclean spirit for all eternity." She will need to say it with each cross she plunges down. The anointing with oil was just something Madame Styvia did believing it would make it stronger. When Sarah asked how many she needed to put in the ground, Madame Styvia said, as many as you can.

"Well, Sister," Abaddon's voiced sizzled. "What are you waiting on?"

"I need my hands," she said.

"Okay."

She felt water droplets hitting her bare arms, stinging the cuts and scrapes she had suffered during the fight. Both hands reached up and grabbed the cross still hanging around her neck and recited, "Blessed are you, Lord, Almighty God, who deigned to bless us in Christ, the living water of our salvation, and to reform us interiorly, grant that we who are fortified by the sprinkling of or use of this water, the youth of the spirit being renewed by the power of the Holy Spirit, may walk always in newness of life." Then she raised her hands up, while reciting, "Lord give me the power to seal this beast. Allow me to use your symbols of the crucifixion to renew and restore our faith in you..." Every cross, broken and unbroken, rose up from the ground. They hung in the air as the rain fell and the lightning struck. Her hands directed them over to the hill where they had spent years standing guard, and with a single drop of her arms, all but one crashed into the ground with a mighty flash. The ground shook, but Abaddon kept Sarah standing. Around them cracks sealed, fire disappeared, and the great gouge that was the hill closed with the walkway leading up like a giant zipper, and looking like nothing had happened. Above them, the smoke from the fires cleared, allowing the first rays of sun in that day. It was late afternoon, and the rays just cleared the horizon, but they looked brilliant to Sarah as they hit the one cross that still hung in the air.

"Almost done," Sarah said."

"Almost?", asked Abaddon as the last cross turned and shot toward Sarah.

# 14

"I woke up nine days later in a hospital, all bandaged up. Most of the scars from that day are gone, with the exception of the one on my chest." Sarah told Ralph. "Mind you, I won't show that scar. I am rather modest about any exposures of the flesh. That scar and the anguish I feel for the loss of Father Lucian have stayed with me until this day."

"That's all right, Sister. How bad were the injuries?"

"Well," Sarah said as she recalled them in her mind. "Several dozen scratches and scrapes. Sorry, I can't remember the exact number anymore. A broken right femur that I was told happened during the struggle with Madame Styvia, Lord Negiev, and Sisters Cecelia and Angelica as they retook control, and three broken ribs and a collapsed lung from when I tried to take control."

"So, it was a battle to bring you back?", Ralph asked. With his hand, he signaled for Kenneth to zoom in tighter for this dramatic question.

"I was told it took three days. I don't remember any of it, and they never told me anything about it," She leaned forward. Her expression and tone turned serious. "You see, it is best not to tell someone what they did when they didn't have control. The guilt can be paralyzing and devastating. It is why to this day, I still don't know what happened there or at Miller's Crossing, and I have stopped asking." Her look and tone were a message that she hoped Ralph and Kenneth both understood. She looked at her brother, who was nodding his agreement to the message.

"I completely understand," Ralph said.

"The person's mental health is as important as their faith," Sarah added.

"I do have some follow-ups. Details, that I want to get right in my notes. Things that if I messed up in the documentary, we will be ridiculed about." Ralph said. He flipped to an empty page in his notepad and gripped the pencil at the ready to jot her answers down. "You mentioned the rite to relock the seal involved soaking the cross in holy water and then putting it into the ground. First, did you take a vial out there with you? Second, how many crosses did you actually do that with?"

"Why, all of them," Sarah said, answering the second question first.

"All of them?," Ralph asked, perplexed. The pencil remained still in his hand. "Weren't there thousands?"

"More than ten thousand, I believe, and I used them all."

Ralph's pencil made its trek back behind his ear as he looked on, confused. "Sister, how did you cover all ten thousand or more crosses in holy water so quick? Or did this really take days to do?"

"Ralph, I consecrated the rain, then drove all but one of them into the ground to relock the seal. The last one, I drove into my chest to try to take care of Abaddon, and myself. A move he hasn't forgiven me for yet. I only wished my aim was better. We would have avoided the dark days that were ahead."

Nope, but I will tell you who it wasn't. It wasn't Marjorie Rawlings. I am sure you figured that out on your own. It also wasn't her husband, Norton Baskin. Whether or not any of the rumors, or any part of the story about them is true, I don't know. He was an unrelated man, a married man, an important man, who was at their hotel for an encounter with his girlfriend. A woman who had a moment of conscience and thought better of their relationship, and refused him. Hearing the word "No", was not something he was used to."

## *Have you read the whole Miller's Crossing series?*

**Miller's Crossing Book 1 – The Ghosts of Miller's Crossing**

Amazon US

Amazon UK

**Ghosts and demons openly wander around the small town of Miller's Crossing. Over 250 years ago, the Vatican assigned a family to be this town's "keeper" to protect the realm of the living from their "visitors". There is just one problem. Edward Meyer doesn't know that is his family, yet.**

Tragedy struck Edward twice. The first robbed him of his childhood and the truth behind who and what he is. The second, cost him his wife, sending him back to Miller's Crossing to start over with his two children.

What he finds when he returns is anything but what he expected. He is thrust into a world that is shocking and mysterious, while also answering and great many questions. With the help of two old friends, he rediscovers who and what he is, but he also discovers another truth, a dark truth. The truth behind the very tragedy that took so much from him. Edward faces a choice. Stay, and take his place in what destiny had planned for him,or run, leaving it and his family's legacy behind.

**Miller's Crossing Book 2 – The Demon of Miller's Crossing**

Amazon US

Amazon UK

**The people of Miller's Crossing believed the worst of the "Dark Period" they had suffered through was behind them, and life had returned to normal. Or, as normal as life can be in a place where it is normal to see ghosts walking around. What they didn't know was the evil entity that tormented them was merely lying in wait.**

After a period of thirty dark years, Miller's Crossing had now enjoyed eight years of peace and calm, allowing the scars of the past to heal. What no one realizes is under the surface the evil entity that caused their pain and suffering is just waiting to rip those wounds open again. Its instrument for destruction will be an unexpected, familiar, and powerful force in the community.

**Miller's Crossing Book 3 – The Exorcism of Miller's Crossing – Available Fall 2020**

Amazon US

Amazon UK

**The "Dark Period" the people of Miller's Crossing suffered through before was nothing compared to life as a hostage to a malevolent demon that is after revenge. Worst of all, those assigned to protect them from such evils are not only helpless, but they are tools in the creatures plan. Extreme measures will be needed, but at what cost.**

The rest of the "keepers" from the remaining 6 paranormal places in the world are called in to help free the people of Miller's Crossing from a demon that has exacted its revenge on the very family assigned to protect them. Action must be taken to avoid losing the town, and allowing the world of the dead to roam free to take over the dominion of the living. This demon took Edward's parents from him while he was a child. What will it take now?

**Miller's Crossing - Prequel – The Origins of Miller's Crossing**
Amazon US
Amazon UK
**There are six known places in the world that are more "paranormal" than anywhere else. The Vatican has taken care to assign "sensitives" and "keepers" to each of those to protect the realm of the living from the realm of the dead. With the colonization of the New World, a seventh location has been found, and time for a new recruit.**

William Miller is a simple farmer in the 18th century coastal town of St. Margaret's Hope Scotland. His life is ordinary and mundane, mostly. He does possess one unique skill. He sees ghosts.

A chance discovery of his special ability exposes him to an organization that needs people like him. An offer is made, he can stay an ordinary farmer, or come to the Vatican for training to join a league of "sensitives" and "keepers" to watch over and care for the areas where the realm of the living and the dead interaction. Will he turn it down, or will he accept and prove he has what it takes to become one of the true legends of their order? It is a decision that can't be made lightly, as there is a cost to pay for generations to come.

# WHAT DID YOU THINK OF THE STORIES OF SISTER SARAH?

*First of all, thank you for purchasing The Stories of Sister Sarah: The Unholy Trinity – Vol 1. I know you could have picked any number of books to read, but you picked this book and for that I am extremely grateful.*

*I hope that it provided you a few moments of enjoyment. If so, it would be really nice if you could share this book with your friends and family by posting to* ***Facebook*** *and* ***Twitter****.*

*If you enjoyed this book and found some benefit in reading this, I'd like to hear from you and hope that you could take some time to post a review on Amazon. Your feedback and support will help this author to greatly improve his writing craft for future projects and make this book even better.*

*You can follow this link to The Stories of Sister Sarah: The Unholy Trinity – Vol 1 now.*

# ALSO BY DAVID CLARK

## *Want more frights?*

**Ghost Storm – Available Now**

Amazon US

Amazon UK

**There is nothing natural about this hurricane. An evil shaman unleashes a super-storm powered by an ancient Amazon spirit to enslave to humanity. Can one man realize what is important in time to protect his family from this danger?**

Successful attorney Jim Preston hates living in his late father's shadow. Eager to leave his stress behind and validate his hard work, he takes his family on a lavish Florida vacation. But his plan turns to dust when a malicious shaman summons a hurricane of soul-stealing spirits.

Though his skeptical lawyer mind disbelieves at first, Jim can't ignore the warnings when the violent wraiths forge a path of destruction. But after numerous unsuccessful escape attempts, his only hope of protecting his wife and children is to confront an ancient demonic force head-on... or become its prisoner.

Can Jim prove he's worth more than a fancy house or car and stop a brutal spectral horde from killing everything he holds dear?

## *Have you read them all?*

### *Game Master Series*

**Book One - Game Master – Game On**

This fast-paced adrenaline filled series follows Robert Deluiz and his friends behind the veil of 1's and 0's and into the underbelly of the online universe where they are trapped as pawns in a sadistic game show for their very lives. Lose a challenge, and you die a horrible death to the cheers and profit of the viewers. Win them all, and you are changed forever.

Can Robert out play, outsmart, and outlast his friends to survive and be crowned Game Master?

Buy book one, Game Master: Game On and see if you have what it takes to be the Game Master.

Available now on Amazon and Kindle Unlimited

**Book Two - Game Master – Playing for Keeps**

The fast-paced horror for Robert and his new wife, Amy, continue. They think they have the game mastered when new players enter with their own set of rules, and they have no intention of playing fair. Motivated by anger and money, the root of all evil, these individuals devise a plan a for the Robert and his friends to repay them. The price... is their lives.

Game Master Play On is a fast-paced sequel ripped from today's headlines. If you like thriller stories with a touch of realism and a stunning twist that goes back to the origins of the Game Master show itself, then you will love this entry in David Clark's dark web trilogy, Game Master.

Buy book two, Game Master: Playing for Keeps to find out if the SanSquad survives.

Available now on Amazon and Kindle Unlimited

**Book Three - Game Master – Reboot**

With one of their own in danger, Robert and Doug reach out to a few of the games earliest players to mount a rescue. During their efforts, Robert finds himself immersed in a Cold War battle to save their friend. Their adversary... an ex-KGB super spy, now turned arms dealer, who is considered one of the most dangerous men walking the planet. Will the skills Robert has learned playing the game help him in this real world raid? There is no trick CGI or trap doors here, the threats are all real.

Buy book three, Game Master: Reboot to read the thrilling conclusion of the Game Master series.

Available now on Amazon and Kindle Unlimited

## *Highway 666 Series*

**Book One – Highway 666**

A collection of four tales straight from the depths of hell itself. These four tales will take you on a high-speed chase down Highway 666, rip your heart out, burn you in a hell, and then leave you feeling lonely and cold at the end.

Stories Include:

- Highway 666 - The fate of three teenagers hooked into a demonic ride-share.
- Till Death – A new spin on the wedding vows
- Demon Apocalypse - It is the end of days, but not how the Bible described it.
- Eternal Journey - A young girl is forever condemned to her last walk, her journey will never end

Available now on Amazon and Kindle Unlimited

**Book Two – The Splurge**

A collection of short stories that follows one family through a dysfunctional Holiday Season that makes the Griswold's look like a Norman Rockwell painting.

Stories included:

- Trick or Treat – The annual neighborhood Halloween decorating contest is taken a bit too far and elicits some unwilling volunteers.
- Family Dinner – When your immediate family abandons you on Thanksgiving, what do you do? Well, you dig down deep on the family tree.
- The Splurge – This is a "Purge" parody focused around the First Black Friday Sale.
- Christmas Eve Nightmare – The family finds more than a Yule log in the fireplace on Christmas Eve

Available now on Amazon and Kindle Unlimited

Cover designed by Eye Creation



David Clark
Visit my website at www.authordavidclark.com

Printed in the United States of America

First Printing: May 2021

Printed in Great Britain
by Amazon